Y0-BFI-459

"This is a story I felt compelled to tell. . . .

"Most of the events and happenings herein are true; or could have been true. . . . I relied mostly on memories, which are not always reliable.

"By today's standards this book may seem 'square' and sentimental—so be it. Perhaps in these troubled times with emphasis on sex, violence, sadism, and perversion, we need some oases that provide happiness, relaxation, peace of mind, and a faith in goodness and human decency."

ESTHER PENCE GARBER

BUTTON SHOES

Esther Pence Garber

THE BRETHREN PRESS ☰ ELGIN, ILLINOIS

BUTTON SHOES

Published by Pillar Books for The Brethren Press

Brethren Press edition published December 1975

Copyright © 1975 by Esther Pence Garber

All Rights Reserved

ISBN: 0–87178–121–2

Printed in the United States of America

The Brethren Press
1451 Dundee Avenue
Elgin, Illinois 60120

To Mary Katherine, my daughter and only child, who never experienced the delights and dilemmas of a family of brothers and sisters.

CONTENTS

NORTH

TO TIMBER RIDGE

THE PENCE HOUSE

THE OLD CLUB

TO SMITH HOUSE

THE BIG OAK

TO MILL CREEK

FRANCES DIEHL'S HOUSE

THE BIG SYCAMORE

THE BLUFF

THE CREEK

THE BOWMAN HOUSE

TO SUNNYSIDE

Drawing by Kermon Thomason

PREFACE

This is a story I felt compelled to tell. It is a story that was lived in the early nineteen-hundreds on a farm in a Dutch community located in the Shenandoah Valley of Virginia. A story of eleven children who with their pappy and mother were, to a great degree, a social and economic entity.

Most of the events and happenings herein are true; or could have been true. Any embellishments or fictional aspects are designed to make it come alive for the reader. Times, dates, names, and chronological order may not be totally accurate; it was not my purpose to make them so. I relied mostly on memories, which are not always reliable. Many of the old ballads and hymns found herein are also a product of memories, thus I cannot attest to their total accuracy. But what is total accuracy in treasures passed from generation to generation, often by word of mouth? We have recorded the lyrics and melodies as we remember them. Only those songs that were not found in any current collections or those with definite variations in lyrics and melodies were used.

It has been with the help of my living brothers and sisters and the neighbors of the orbit in which we moved that I have been able to recall many of the events of those past years, so to them I say, *"Danke schee."*

I am beholden to others who inspired and encouraged, edited and corrected. But most of all to my husband Bill, who not only patiently permitted me to neglect my house-wifely duties, but served as my sounding board and critic. He also assumed the difficult task of writing the music to many of the old songs and ballads found herein, transcribing these tunes and lyrics to a large degree from the memory of my sister Bertha. Again, *"Danke schee."*

By today's standards this book may seem "square" and sentimental—so be it. Perhaps in these troubled times with emphasis on sex, violence, sadism, and perversion, we need some oases that provide happiness, relaxation, peace of mind, and a faith in goodness and human decency.

Chapter 1

STRAWBERRY SHORTCAKE

"Girr-r-lls! Esther! Frances! Supper's ready! Come to supper right away!" It was a hot day early in summer, 90° in the shade of the big, black-bottomed, applebutter kettle hanging on its wooden peg by the washhouse door. The voice coming from the farmhouse kitchen was Mother's, calling all the young Pence flock from their various activities of work and play on the farm to the evening meal.

Up Frances and I jumped from our own special corner in the yard under the pear trees. Here we had been marking off in the dirt the rooms in our dream house with a few twigs and one broken-handled spoon. Brushing the dust from the fronts of our dresses with dustier hands, we ran past the snowball bush, around the back of the house, past the grape arbor over the cistern to the back porch that led into the kitchen.

"Girls, wash your dirty hands, and then, Esther, you run to the barn and tell the men supper is ready."

I dipped out one dipper of water from the bucket that sat in the rectangular iron sink in the corner of the kitchen behind the porch door. Ere now, we had learned to use the water as sparingly as possible, for when the bucket was emptied, it might mean that anyone of us would be the appointed person to go to the cistern, pump a fresh bucketful, and carry it back into the house. Sometimes, if we were lucky and the wind blew enough to turn the windmill, we could possibly get a small stream of water

11

from the spigot to slowly fill the bucket. But this was not a dependable source as we soon learned.

After a rather limited amount of swishing hands in the same pan of water, we reached for the towel on its wooden roller fastened on the back of the door, looking for the one dry spot that was never quite there. This towel had no stopping point, but went round and round, being used over and over, until Mother decided it was sufficiently dirty to require a new one.

My fast wash over, I dashed toward the barn where the men, boys included, were finishing the evening chores of feeding and bedding down the horses and cows for the night. As the toughened soles of my bare feet flew along, they were not aware of the hardened earth that stretched from the house to the barn; earth that was as hard as the mortar in the stone wall beneath the red frame barn I was approaching; hardened from the years in which human feet, animal hoofs, and the wheels of farm machinery had crisscrossed it innumerable times. At that moment, feet were a part of the rhythm of a free moving body, a body of which one is hardly aware as it moves about familiar places. At that moment, too, the thoughts that were tripping happily in my head were totally removed from all consciousness of the physical, for we were having the best of all possible treats for supper—fresh wild strawberry shortcake!

The morning had brought forth a suggestion from Mother that we all accepted with little grumbling: "If you children would like to go and see if you can find some strawberries before it gets so hot, I'll make a strawberry shortcake for supper."

Quickly we had finished up the morning farm chores: bedmaking, dishwashing, milking, feeding the cats, and sweeping out the dining room and kitchen. Almost before the last bit of dew had left the patches and fence rows where we would search for the bright red berries, we were ready to set out. The chosen ones this day were Mary, fourth daughter down the ladder and the third one up, and Wilbur and Jacob, the two youngest boys, each with a half gallon tin molasses bucket. Then, there were Frances and

I, the two youngest in the family of eleven living children, Frances being the fat happy baby. She and I each carried a pint tin cup, as we were not expected to accomplish as much as the older ones. But training in all the chores on our eighty-acre farm began early for each little Pence as he occupied his place in the family lineup. It may seem strange to our sophisticates of today, but the challenge to accomplish in these ordinary tasks was there—even to picking a small tin cup of strawberries full to the brim!

So, up the dusty road we trudged, searching the weeds along the fence rows as we went, weeds that were still wet from the early morning's dew where the sun's rays had not penetrated. Picking handfuls as we moved along, the buckets ever so slowly began to fill. Sometimes, the patches extended beyond the fence and into the fields. However, fences were no barrier as any farm kid knew, so each time over we would go. Backs were tired; fingers were red and sticky; and the sun was hot before Mary, Wilbur, and Jake had just about filled their buckets. And my cup was so full that I had to hold it firmly with both hands and walk very carefully, lest I spill some of my precious berries! And Frances—what about Frances?

Mary, checking on her accomplishments, asked, "Why didn't you pick anymore than that, Frances?" The bottom of her cup was scarcely covered.

"She hasn't done anything all morning but just sit around," answered Wilbur, whose tolerance of small sisters was rather modest.

"I know what! She ate them as fast as she picked them. Look at her mouth—it's all red!" I added.

Frances sheepishly explained, "I couldn't find hardly any." Having said this, she rubbed the red telltale lips with her little grubby hand. Over the years as we looked back, we realized this first little event was typical of Frances, for we came to know her as the one who loved to eat more than she liked to participate in other activities.

We had not gone far on our way home when we met our neighbor friends: Frances Diehl, and Margaret and Elizabeth Bowman, who were such an important part of our lives in this Shenandoah Valley community. They, too, were on a berry picking errand. In those days fence rows and fields were open to all. There were no "No Trespassing!" or "Private! Keep Out!" signs to be found on any farm. This was indeed true freedom. It was the Biblical gleaning concept still alive and practiced in the twentieth century.

Joining company and chatter, we automatically stopped under the shade of the old gnarled cedar tree that stood at the crossroads where to us all roads met. For all the years we lived in this spot, this crossroads and this cedar tree were the landmark for many meetings and many farewells, and they have etched themselves in our memories for all the years that have followed. The main road led to the little white wooden church where we worshiped on Sunday afternoons in our very young years. In the opposite direction it led "up the road" two miles to the two-story frame school where we said our "Wills and Mays" instead of "Dicks and Janes." Intersecting this was the road that went by the Pence house a few hundred yards away. This merged at the crossing with a lane that led to the Showalter farm where Frances Diehl lived with her grandmother and uncle. From thence, the Bowman home was reached by a path that led up a steep hill. These three farms were home to all the Bowmans, the Pences, and Frances Diehl, and were the settings for many gatherings and great merriment for all the days and years of our childhood.

This day, everyone took only a few minutes to wipe the sweat and to cool off, and to compare the fruits of our morning's work. Then, since our timepieces—our stomachs—told us it was getting near dinner time: we said our "goodbyes"; "come down to see us this afternoons"; "it's your turns"; over and over, as was our wont to do, and we all went our separate ways.

After dinner, the biggest meal of the day on a farm, Pappy and the four boys returned to the barn and fields to resume the work for the afternoon. We girls carried the dishes to the kitchen for washing in the big tin dishpan filled with warm water and a chunk of homemade soap.

At length, the time for preparing the strawberries for

our shortcake was at hand. Mother, Bertha, Ruth, Elizabeth, and Mary carried dining room chairs to the kitchen porch on which to sit. This porch was the place for many chores to be performed, since it took one away from the hot kitchen and to the outdoors, which is a part of life itself to all farm people. There were clean crocks to put the berries in after capping, and each person had a bowl or pan of water on her lap for the process. This sitting work was a sort of rest period for the day; we had not yet conceived of "nap times" or "coffee breaks"— at least not in this community. The labor at the farm was seldom interrupted or finished until the sun went down behind the mountains to the west of us.

At this age of our lives, Frances and I sat on the edge of the low porch and slithered our toes around in the cool grass. Occasionally there was an errand to run such as: "Empty my bowl of caps in the slop bucket for me, Esther," or "Frances, bring me a dipper of water." But mostly, we sat and listened contentedly to the talk between mother and daughters. Listening to the conversation of grown-ups was one of my favorite pastimes, which on occasions earned me the title of "Nosy" or "Little Pitcher with Big Ears"; especially when the subject of the conversation was not meant for little folk to hear.

"Girls, let's sing for a little. I love to hear you," Mother suggested. If practice produced good singers, we should have been famous. However, there were no prospective prima donnas in our family. But we did love to sing; and when healthy young voices do so for joy and pleasure, it at least makes a pretty sound. So sing we did, lustily and often.

"Let's sing the 'Banks of Cloudy.'* I don't know all the verses yet, and I'd like to learn them," Mary requested.

"Start us off, Bertha. I think you know it better than anyone else," said Mother.

By the time we had sung all twelve verses, and the wayward young man had returned to the arms of his sweet-

*Glossary

15

heart and vowed to be faithful forever, I sighed with relief at the happy ending to such a moving, almost tragedy.

But now, the preparation of the bright red berries and the cleaning up after was completed. Everyone automatically moved into the kitchen; Mother to begin work on the marvelous shortcake dough, a procedure (not a recipe) that had been passed from Dutch mothers to their daughters for untold generations. I have ofttimes wished I were able to pass this process on to my daughter and to succeeding generations, but somewhere the skill has been lost: perhaps, in cake mixes that come in boxes or biscuits that come in cans; perhaps, because we no longer have in abundance the rich cream and butter that is so much a part of Dutch cooking; perhaps, because we no longer have big black ovens heated by a wood-burning stove, ovens that had no thermometers but whose temperature was tested only by the feel of the hand. I rather believe, though, that the success was more than likely due to a sort of magic that Mother put into it with her plump, hardworking hands and a heart of love for her family.

Elizabeth was at Mother's elbow to help in this preparation, for she was the eldest daughter and more interested in the art of cooking and housekeeping, as a proper young woman of the day should be.

The dough they made was a great hunk of soft rich pastry, rather like a biscuit mix. Dividing it into halves, Mother rolled out one portion and fitted it into a large black bread pan, approximately fourteen by twenty inches, to make a shell. Then, over this was spread rather generously some nice soft butter. The other half was then rolled out and laid carefully on top of the first. Now all was ready for baking in the oven whose heat Mother had first properly tested with her hand.

In the meantime, Bertha, Ruth, and Mary were making other preparations for supper. Bertha was adding a generous portion of sugar to the berries in a large crock and was mashing them with the wooden potato masher.

"Can I mash a little, Bertha?" I asked.

"Me too, me too!" Frances chimed in.

16

Bertha indulged us for a minute, knowing full well that in the process we would probably manage to get our fingers down in the mixture, to lick them off afterwards.

At this time, Ruth and Mary were setting the table and getting other things out of the safe for supper. They carefully took the huge Sunday meat platter, with a deep blue design around the edge, to the kitchen for the shortcake. Since the simple chores had been finished, Frances and I took ourselves to our special corner in the yard to play for the minutes left us.

Now that supper was about ready and Mother had told me to call the menfolks, there I was, gladly on my way to the barn to make this announcement. Into the lower door I darted. "Pappy! Jasper! Charlie!" I called. "Mother said to tell you that supper is ready!"

Jasper answered, "We'll be along in a minute. We are just finishing up."

Above us, we could hear Jake and Wilbur laughing and tussling in the hay mow; so up the stairs to the main floor of the barn I quickly went.

"Wilbur! Jake! Supper's ready!"

Down the pile of hay they slid, tufts of the dry sweet grass clinging to their shirts and overalls and no doubt seeds in their ears and hair.

Wilbur challenged, "I'll beat ya' to the house."

"I'll betcha' can't," countered Jake, and off they raced, big bare feet flying to be the first to the wash pan.

By the time Pappy, Jasper, and Charlie had arrived at the house, Mother had removed the shortcake dough, which was "done," from the oven. Then after placing the bottom layer on the meat plate, she dipped on many ladles of strawberries and followed with the top layer and the remainder of the berries.

After much scrambling and hurrying, everyone was properly washed for the evening meal—at least that was the assumption.

Pappy sat at the head of the long family table; to his right, on a bench almost as long as the table, sat the boys in chronological order: Jasper, Charlie, Wilbur, and Jacob. On his left sat Mother, then the girls in the same order:

17

Elizabeth, Bertha, having moved up a notch in Grace's absence, Ruth, and Mary. Lastly, at the foot directly facing Pappy, some distance away on a small bench perched Frances and I. We always sat close together on this bench for if one or the other chanced to move too near the end, it had a tendency to tilt. One or two upsetting experiences and that lesson was learned. Sitting at the bottom of this long line at the table wasn't usually very profitable, but at other times being the youngest in the family did have its advantages.

Whether this seating arrangement conformed to the old Biblical patriarchal system is questionable, but Pappy, at least, had his own little modified patriarchal order.

When all were settled at the table, Pappy said, "Let's bow our heads.

> Our kind Father in heaven, we thank Thee for the many blessings of life. Bless this food to its intended use and our lives to Thy service. Pardon us of our many wrongs and in death save us for Christ's sake.
>
> Amen."

Then Mother, knowing how hungry everyone was, quickly and expertly divided the shortcake into twelve unequal portions, the larger for the older ones, especially the men; but none went without enough to satisfy his tummy's desires. No president or secretary of state had ever dined on more delectable food!

For a time, the only sound to be heard was the clicking of spoons and forks on the plates. But twelve people, and mostly youngsters, are not apt to keep the silence for long.

"Gee, Mother, this sure is good! Can we have another one if we pick some more berries?"

"I'll go again tomorrow."

"Boys, I think Red Cow is ready to drop her 'hammi'* (calf) by tomorrow so we won't take her out to pasture in the morning."

---

*Commonly spelled 'hommy'

"I hope it's a girl hammi. Girls are better than boys."

"I don't, 'cause if it's a girl, when she grows up we'll have to milk her."

"Wilbur is pushing me off the bench!"

"You started it, Jake!"

"I did not, Wilbur, you did!"

"Boys, leave the table."

Since the two had finished their shortcake, they got up from the bench without too many regrets, but still peeved with each other because they had not gotten by with their shenanigans. They lumbered out into the yard where they continued their pushing and shoving, their tussling and "hassling."

"Frances, don't lick your plate like that!"

"Well, girls, I guess it's time to clean up the table."

Day was ending and twilight was making silhouettes of the landscape around us—the trees and farm buildings, the fences and rolling fields—as we settled down on the front porch for a bit of relaxation and rest before turning in for the night. Mother and Pappy sat in the two rockers; Bertha, Ruth, and Mary sat on the edge of the porch, feet dangling; Elizabeth, Jasper, and Charlie were relaxing on the steps. Wilbur and Jake, their energy spent, and Frances and I lay flat on our backs in the cool grass. We watched the millions of stars twinkling in the sky above us, as twilight turned into dark. The lightning bugs—the little lamplighters of the night—flitted around us, their lights twinkling, too, as if to challenge the stars above them for their place in the universe. Then the darkness fell softly, silently. It enfolded and embraced us, 'til we, too, were one with the great universe around us.

CHAPTER 2

QUILT SQUARES

Life for me began at about the age of three when I became aware that I had a rugged six-foot father (Pappy) with white hair, a full white beard, and eyes as blue as the sky on a clear day. His face was patterned with lines —good lines, beautiful lines, etched there by the sun, the wind, and the cold of our valley. There were smile and laughter lines, too, engraved by the aliveness and effervescence of a brood of eleven living children.

And there was Mother—short, fat, rotund, and so typically Dutch. Her hair was parted in the middle and combed around to be caught in a bun at the back of her head, exposing a gentle face dominated by large hazel eyes. Pappy said that when she was young, she was the prettiest girl in the neighborhood, and always added, "She still is." Who could possibly disagree?

Then, there was Lizzie Flora, the first born. By the time I was three and old enough to be aware of people and places, Lizzie had gone out into the world to pursue her chosen profession, teaching in public school. My memories of her were formed on weekends and summers when she came home to be with the family. We were always glad to have her back among us to talk about her work and to help at the farm. Lizzie, later Elizabeth, was pretty and proud—too proud to be called the undignified name of Lizzie.

Grace Arlene—Grace possessed what young farm girls can only dream about. She was already married to a handsome dentist, had a home in the big city of Baltimore, and had been to places and had seen things that we could not envision even in our dreams. So Grace, too, was rather on the periphery of my farm experiences.

Jasper Harshbarger—Jasper was always the quiet thoughtful one, grown up beyond his years, taking on responsibilities at an early age. Perhaps, the rugged and vigorous farm life of those early times often demanded that, especially of the eldest son in the family. He had stopped going to school in his early teens to become Pappy's right hand man on the farm; and besides, he never seemed to enjoy school anyhow.

Then came Charles Joseph—Charlie was born full of merriment and foolishness mixed with not a small amount of deviltry. He often kept us in stitches with his humor and his puckish tricks. Even as he grew older, he never took life very seriously, and went out into the world at a rather early age to seek his fortune. But home seemed to pull him back for many visits with us to the delight of all.

And Bertha Ola—Bertha and Charlie were not twins, but at least they must have been born under the same sign of the Zodiac, for she, too, was high-spirited and full of mirth. Between the two of them, they kept things rather lively around the farm. Coupled with this, however, as she matured, was a serious nature, and Mother depended on her often to help supervise and guide her younger brothers and sisters. Later she pursued her chosen career with vigor and determination. She, too, became a teacher.

Ruth Magdalene—By this time, someone must have decided that Mother and Pappy needed a break, a respite from the high spirits of the former two, for Ruth was gentle, sweet, and modest. In fact, a bit more than modest, she was shy, so shy that she blushed at almost any provocation. The blush made her even more beautiful on the outside, but less comfortable on the inside.

Mary Hope—I wonder why there is one in every family that the rest like to tease? In ours it was Mary. As she grew up, however, she took her rightful place beside us, and sometimes against us. She loved pretty clothes, and generally managed to get whatever her older sisters, Elizabeth, Bertha, and Ruth acquired, whether it was a new dress or a pair of laced, white, high-top shoes.

Wilbur Samuel and Jacob David were typical pre-puberty boys—obstreperous, bullyish, pesky, contrary, and "lubbardy" (clumsy)—what other adjectives do you apply to boys of that age? They loved to tease their two little sisters, and I guess we loved it, too. Isn't it strange how one feels disgust and love for members of his own family at the same time? That sums up how we all felt about our two young brothers.

James Harold—Born January 14, 1909; Died June 30, 1909.

Esther Virginia—What about me? I'll assign to you the prerogative to form your own judgment and characterization of me as you read my story.

At last, Frances Ellen—She was the happy, placid, curly-headed baby of our family. She mostly liked to sit around, laugh and gurgle, and grow fat. She would enter into activities with me after a little urging and prodding. We were not far apart in age and so we spent many happy childhood hours together.

Fall had come late this year, which was a beneficent gift for the family table. We had not had a heavy frost until October, so the garden had yielded many late vegetables: corn, tomatoes, and a scattering of beans on the vines. This was a windfall indeed to farm diets of those times which were rather limited in fresh fruits and vegetables. But the last few days had brought a real change in the weather—temperatures had dropped rather significantly in a short interval—so we knew that fall was here, finally, unequivocally, permanently. The garden, which had a few short days earlier given us some unexpected bonuses, was now limp and black from the ferocity of the two mornings of hoarfrost. The dry brown cornstalks flapped in the breeze like so many abandoned scarecrows, and about as lifeless. If there were any fruit left on the tomato plants, it was now squashy and rotten, preparing to return to the soil that had produced it.

Over the fields, the crows were sneaking in and out of

the corn rows, searching for one last meal from the piles of shucked ripened corn by the fodder shocks before the farmer hauled it into the corn crib for the winter or before it was covered completely by some early snowfall. Their raucous calls sounded more harsh and dissonant than ever in the bitter fall winds.

The night before, all were huddled around the warm black stove in the living room reluctant to leave its warmth hoping to absorb one last ray of heat before we made off to jump between cold bed covers in our unheated rooms upstairs. In these last scurrying minutes we received a weather bulletin by way of a quiet announcement from Mother, "It's going to be mighty raw weather tomorrow, I'm afraid. Children, get out your long underwear to put on when you get up in the morning. You will be needing it."

Moans and groans all around.

"Aw, do we have to?"

"Can't we wait a little bit longer?"

"They itch me! I can't stand it!"

"My flap won't ever stay buttoned!"

"Mine are gittin' too short, can't Jake wear 'em?"

Most of these expressed feelings came from us younger ones; the older children, from more years of experience than ours, knew the answer that would surely be forthcoming, and they had learned to accept the inevitable. Yes, Mother was adamant. They had also learned, like it or not, that the warmth from this apparel was necessary to protect them against the cold of farmhouses, schoolhouses, and churches, heated only by wood or coal stoves; and from the cold they must endure while performing the many outdoor farm chores.

After all these complaints were made, Mother turned to Frances and me. "Girls, I have a little patching and darning to do yet on your suits. I guess you'll have to wait a coupl'a days to put them on. I think that will be all right, since you don't have to be out in the cold so much like the others."

"Oh goody! Goody!"

The next morning, everyone ran down the backstairs

at breakneck speed—you guessed it—the older children in long underwear, to dress by the warm fire that Pappy had already started in the stove. They resembled a team of gymnasts in long trousers and long sleeve shirts, and just as active as they jumped and hopped around each other, trying to get near the stove.

Wilbur's efforts at this proved too fruitful, for at that moment he gave forth with a terrific howl, "Ouw-w, ou-u-w! I burn't myself!" and the tears flowed.

Bertha, consolingly said, "Let me see what you did."

There branded on his bare bottom, exposed by the non-zippered cleavage of his underwear was a pink, not quite complete imprint of the name plate on the stove, "Cole's Hot——"

Mother immediately spread the burn with a generous amount of applebutter, and added her inexhaustible supply of sympathy as she dried his tears.

Then began the task that made us hate long underwear with vehemence: that of trying to fold over the bottoms of the legs so that they fitted neatly and smoothly into our long, black, ribbed stockings, with no lumps showing above our high top shoes. If you have never attempted this, you cannot imagine the skill it takes to fold over, hold, and pull up the stockings all in one motion. I don't remember that any of us ever became professional at this, for it always seemed that there was a prolonged doing and redoing before satisfactory results were achieved. If you were a child of the seventies suddenly transported back to those days, you might have wondered why all youngsters had lumps on the sides of both legs.

While we were all scrambling to get into our clothes, Mother was already in the kitchen getting the range heated and preparing to fry mush in a long shallow oval skillet that covered two holes on the stove. That and cane molasses would be our breakfast for the morning, as it was on frequent occasions. Bertha and Ruth hurried to the barn to do the morning's milking, as this was a school day and a reasonably early start was needed to walk the two miles and be at school on time. On this particular week, Bertha and Ruth were responsible for the milking job in the mornings, Mary and Wilbur in the evenings; the following week this arrangement would be reversed. The time came, when Frances and I had to learn and perform this task.

As I look back to those days, I believe we all shared a common feeling about milking—no one cherished doing the job, thus no one could be bribed to do it for another. We all had to simply take our turns at a task that was cold in the winter, and unpleasant in summer when the "old cow" would swish her tail at the flies and frequently slap us across the face in the process.

"But you must take the bitter with the sweet," Mother and Pappy always said.

The hustle and bustle of the morning had about ceased, when Mother turned to those who were soon to leave for school. "Children, I think you'd better be on your way now, so you won't be late for school. Esther and Frances can help me with the dishes and brushing out the crumbs. Boys, be sure your faces and hands are clean."

All hustled into stocking caps, sweaters, jackets; then they picked up their tin lunch pails, which were really converted molasses buckets. These probably contained applebutter or molasses "bread," and hopefully, a piece of pie or a ginger or sugar cookie. Lastly, they slung their book satchels across their shoulders, filled with their books in one end to be balanced by apples in the other end. These book satchels were interesting articles; but the beauty of them could be found only in their usefulness and durability. They were constructed from approximately a yard's length of overall material, stitched all around save an opening in the center on one of the long sides, an opening for shoving in books and apples.

Finally, they were gone; the walls, the doors, and the windows seemed to shake themselves a bit, and then settle down for the day, so as to be ready for the next onslaught.

Frances and I did what we could, in our childish and limited way, to help Mother with the dishes and the sweeping. We were at least six inches taller after she had

25

announced that we would help her do this grown-up's work.

Mother, commending our efforts, said, "Since you girls helped me so nicely, I believe I'll have time to make some *fassnachts* this morning. The children will like them in their school lunch buckets."

These *fassnachts* were almost a counterpart of the modern doughnut, except that Mother cut them square with a knife instead of round with a doughnut cutter; then she cut two slits across them, rather than a hole in the middle, and they were ready for frying. Frances and I were delighted, for we knew there would be some scraps of dough before and after frying—accidentally, intentionally —made available for us to nibble on.

Sis and I were now free to get our heads together and decide on our activities for the morning.

"Let's cut some paper dolls from the catalog. Mother, can we have some shears and a catalog?" I asked.

"There is a Sears Roebuck Catalog on the dining room porch and there's a pair of shears in the bottom sewing machine drawer. Now you girls be careful with those shears," cautioned Mother.

We grew a couple more inches at being allowed to handle a pair of scissors usually reserved for grown-ups.

With catalog and shears in hand, we lay flat on our bellies near the stove in the living room, and began turning to the stiff, slick, colored pages of people in the book that presented a new world of clothes and color to two little farm girls. We never wasted the soft black and white pages in these Sears Roebuck or Montgomery Ward catalogs, for they served a very useful function in the household. They were taken down the chicken yard path to the *scheishaus* (outside toilet) and deposited in a brass bucket for daily, or more accurately, hourly use by the family. When we had torn our way over to the farm machinery pages, we knew it was time for another catalog. The brass bucket once in a lowly place, today, polished to its full brightness, has its place of honor on the hearth in my living room.

26

Frances, turning to me, said, "Let me cut a while, Esther."

"All right, but Mother said be careful; and you are littler than I am."

"Gee, isn't that a pretty green striped dress? I'd like to have one like it!" Frances wishfully exclaimed.

"I'd rather have the blue one; I like blue better."

"Look at that red coat with the fur collar! It looks like old mother cat's fur. It's the same color. You reckon they kill cats and use their fur for things like that? I sure wouldn't want them to find our old mother cat, or Tom either!"

My interest in coats waning, I said, "Let's find the shoes. I love button shoes! I hope Mother will buy me a pair sometime—maybe when I go to school, or when I get a little bigger! I sure like those little buttoners they button them with!"

"I want to live in the city when I get big, that's what I want to do."

The wind interrupted our conversation frequently as it whistled shrilly around the corners of our frame farm house, reminding us again that fall was permanently here. That whistle was an eerie haunting sound, as if some soul from a past time had been reincarnated in the wind and was calling back to a former life lost in some bygone era. It made us feel a little forlorn, and sad, too; and we unconsciously and intuitively drew a bit closer together.

As Mother busied herself with the *fassnachts* in the kitchen, her voice came floating in to the two of us lying on the floor in the front room. Mother often sang at her daily job of homemaking and familycaring. The refrain that came to our ears at this moment was one we had heard her sing at other times, and it added to the sad emotions that we already were feeling. I always felt so sorry for that poor little child. I wanted to weep every time she sang those lyrics.

The Little Orphan Girl*

"No home, no home," cried the little girl,
As she stood at the prince's door.
"Won't you give me a home?" she feebly said.
"A home and a crust of bread?"

"My father, sir, I never knew,"
And the tears in her eyes shone bright,
"My mother, she sleeps in a new-made grave.
'Tis an orphan that begs tonight."

The rich man slept on his velvet bed,
And dreamed of his silver and gold.
But the little girl lay on her bed of snow,
And murmured, "So cold, so cold."

The morning dawned on the little girl,
As she lay at the marble hall.
But her spirit had fled to the mansions above,
Where there's room and bread for all.

By the time Mother had completed these sad lyrics,
Frances and I had decided we were tired of cutting paper
dolls; and perhaps, without being aware, we needed to
change our emotional climate a bit.

"Mother, can Esther and I go out and play in the front
yard awhile? The sun is gettin' nice and warm."

"Yes, for a little while, but be sure to put on your
sweaters and caps. It's not that warm yet, and you don't
have on your long underwear."

We threw the paper scraps into the coal bucket behind
the stove, put the scissors back in their proper place and
the catalog on the dining room porch for future use.
Donning caps and sweaters, we ran out the front door and
into the yard. The wind was still blowing, but it was not
quite so cold now. In the maple tree above our heads, the
wren house looked very empty and forlorn, swaying hither

*Glossary

28

and thither in the breeze, Jenny Wren having long since departed. We found the rakes the boys had left there after raking up the maple leaves the evening before. Then, we began raking the brown dried leaves into little rows, laying out the rooms in a new and bigger dream house— juvenile architects who had never heard of the word. We had doors opening from room to room, so it also served the purpose of allowing us to play tag, which we did for a short time.

Dinner time brought Mother to the door calling us to come in and wash up. Another dream house abandoned and forgotten for another season.

At dinner, Mother had asked Pappy to have Jasper hitch Morg, one of our horses, to the buggy. She wanted to visit her Pap, our Grandpap Harshbarger, who was ill at the time. So it was, that Frances and I were left for the afternoon in Pappy's care, with instructions to be good girls while she was gone. Pappy at that time was secretary and treasurer of the Rockingham Home Mutual Fire Insurance Company which paid him an annual salary of three hundred dollars. This went a long way in helping clothe the family and to buy other necessities. This afternoon, he had work to do on his books and would be indoors to give us supervision.

As I look back, I am not quite sure what prompted the events of that afternoon. Perhaps, Sis and I had developed an interest in cutting and wanted to use the shears some more; or, perhaps, we had seen our sisters cutting quilt squares and wanted to try our skill at this; perhaps, it was a combination of both. At any rate, there we were perched on the sofa in the front room with the big shears in our possession; and there Pappy was in his adjoining bedroom with an open door between, intently occupied with his insurance books spread out before him on a walnut drop-leaf table.

Frances asked, "We don't have any goods, how can we cut quilt squares?"

After a few seconds of searching my mind, which was over-active at times but not always rational, I said, "I know! We can cut off our dress sleeves; they will make nice ones."

Having brought forth this piece of juvenile wisdom, and getting no argument from Frances, who was ever ready to accept her slightly elder sister's suggestions, we carefully took the big shears and proceeded to cut the sleeves from each other's dresses as near to the shoulders as possible. I have wondered many times since how two small girls ever managed this feat without cutting or sticking each other. Now, taking turns, we cut the gingham-checked sleeves into pieces as nearly square as our inexperience would permit.

"I like doing this, don't you?"

"Yeah, this is fun! These are real pretty squares," replied Frances.

"Now, we can do some sewing, too. I bet Mother will let us have a needle and some thread."

At that moment, Pappy, who was tired of book work, wanted a few minutes rest; so he left the bedroom, came out into the living room, and sat down in his special chair in its special place by the window. Casually glancing our way, he inquired, "Girls, what are you doing?"

"Nuthin'."

Accepting our reply without further investigation, he leaned back in his rocker and dozed for a few minutes. Somewhere in the depths of our minds, there must have lurked the feeling that what we were doing might just be wrong; for at that point, we gathered together our paraphernalia, slipped surreptitiously into the bedroom, and sat on the bed to continue our busy work.

"We need some more goods. This is all cut up," said Frances.

Again searching my resourceful (?) mind for a few seconds, I came forth with another bright (?) idea. "Let's take off our drawers and use them; they'll be pretty with the checkered squares."

"I'm scared to do that; Mother might find out!"

"Aw, no she won't," I countered, exposing the reasoning powers of one five year old.

So following through with my suggestion, we proceeded

to take off our drawers—drawers made of brown cotton cloth and fastened to a band around the top that buttoned on one side. Frances, whose tummy had grown a bit bigger than the band, had a string through the buttonhole which looped over the button. This presented a problem for a minute, as she had somehow managed to twist it several times around the button, but we finally succeeded in undoing it.

At that moment, Pappy chose to wake up, and then proceeded back to the bedroom to begin his former task. Glancing at us as before, he again asked, "Girls, what are you doing?"

And again, the same response. "Nuthin'." With that we proceeded to gather up the scissors, our gingham squares, and our uncut drawers and returned to the living room as before—still to be on the safe side.

Pappy continued with his job and we with ours. Cutting through thick heavy double seams and belts at the tops of our drawers, we kept at our tasks with some perseverance. Somewhere along the process of completing our project, the enormity of what we were doing began to slowly penetrate our consciousness. Slowly, it dawned on us that Mother just might find out what we had done—and fear began to set in.

"Esther, I'm scared Mother might find out what we did!"

"I'm scared too; she might get us; she might even spank us! Let's hide our squares somewhere so she won't see them."

"Where can we hide them?"

Again my mind, perhaps less able to function clearly now, did finally come up with what I thought would be a good hiding place. So we hurriedly carried out my idea and packed them away for safe keeping, never to be revealed. Then we picked up all telltale signs of our afternoon's project.

We were still somewhat apprehensive when Mother returned home from her visit, and as our brothers and sisters walked in from school almost simultaneously. With

31

one glance, Mother, of course, noticed our sleeveless apparel.

"Girls, what have you done to your dresses?" she asked very sternly.

No answer.

"Esther, how did you do that, and where are your dress sleeves?" more sternly.

Still no answer.

With that, Mother picked me up and threw me across her lap face downward. This action revealed my bare behind in all its youthful pinkness.

"Girls, where are your britches?" in astonishment.

No answer.

"Where did you put all your things?" in increasing impatience.

Still no answer.

With that unbroken silence, Mother lowered the boom on all that uncovered, quivering bottom with some of the considerable strength she possessed. It was a truly thorough spanking.

Now it was time for Frances to receive the same medicine, who all the while through my chastisement was shedding great tears of sympathy—or apprehension. Even in my own anguish, I sensed that she was not receiving the full measure that I had.

"You spanked me harder than you did Frances!" I bawled.

"You are the oldest and I think you were responsible for this!"

How well she knew her own children! No doubt, Mother was correct in this assumption; but this was little consolation to my hurt feelings, and did nothing to assuage the sting in my painful behind.

In the meantime, Bertha, Ruth, and Mary were searching for the results of our handiwork of the afternoon. They looked under things, on things, in things, and behind things, until at length Mary looked under Mother's and Pappy's bed. With her keen eyes, she became aware that their chamber was pushed way to the backside of their bed into the farthest corner. Her alertness told her that was rather unusual, as, of course, it normally sat handily near the front edge of the bed. She crawled under and pulled the pottie out with her. And there packed neatly and compactly almost to the top were the white and checkered pieces that represented our labors of the afternoon.

We can only conclude that our inability to realize our secret would be discovered when Mother and Pappy would want to use this utensil for the purpose for which it was created, reveals the limits of rationalization of small children. This find swiftly brought the events of the afternoon, and especially the last half hour, to a climax; but it was not yet over for Frances and me as we continued to heave and sob.

Wilbur, with thoughts of our bare buttocks, said, "Mother warmed your britches! Ha! Ha! Ha!"

Jake, following the lead of his older brother, joined in. "Yeah, Mother warmed your britch-e-e-es! Mother warmed your britch-e-e-es! Mother warmed—"

"Boys, go on outdoors and get your work done!" ordered Mother.

"Mother warmed your britch-e-e-es! Mother warmed your—," faded off into nothingness as they took for the outdoors.

Even Bertha, Ruth, and Mary, our own sisters, stood in the corner and giggled with the boys. I imagine, too, that in spite of the seriousness of our actions, Mother must have chuckled inside at the comedy in the whole situation. Our rejection was complete.

Frances and I were rather subdued throughout the evening. For awhile, as others were busy with their evening chores, we sat in the corner of the front room and sulked, indulging in not a little self-pity.

"Nobody likes us anymore."

"And I hate all of them!"

"Let's run away from home."

"Let's do; then they'll be sorry. They'll wish that they hadn't been so mean to us."

Even at the supper table we refused to join in the laughter and merriment, when Bertha reported on Charlie's

33

conduct at school. "Charlie, I nearly died laughing at you and Louie at school today, and so did everybody else."

"Bertha, you talk too much," he accused, but Charlie couldn't conceal his feelings of mirth either, so he began giggling with Bertha.

Jasper prodded, "Tell us about it, Bertha."

Bertha, her appetite whetted for spinning a good story, related, "Somebody brought an old squirrel's tail to school today, and at recess time someone pinned it on Louie Chandler. I think he knew it was there, 'cause when we lined up to come in he was twitching his hips all around. As he walked in the door by the teacher, she noticed the tail and pulled it off with a big angry jerk. When she did this, Charlie yelled, 'Louie, did it hurt?' Everybody busted out laughing, and teacher couldn't keep her face straight either, even if she was disgusted."

Mother and Pappy had to laugh, too, at the little comedy. They joined in with the others, though they often worried about Charlie's conduct and his lack of interest in his work. But seeing the humor in the situation, they let it pass without comment.

Later, when all farm activities had ceased and we sat in the living room, Mother found the time and opportunity to take Frances on one knee and me on the other. She held us gently against her, as she slowly rocked her chair back and forth. She chatted quietly with us about little things that go with little girls. In these last placid moments before bedtime, we knew that Mother was already forgetting the misdeeds of the afternoon, and that she still loved us no matter what.

Somehow though, for a long time to come, I had no desire to cut quilt pieces as my sisters often did when they had spare time, especially the little squares cut to make "nine diamond" comfort tops.

Chapter 3

PAIN—PLEASURE

The winter of 1918–1919 began as any other winter of our lives. The harvesting of crops had been completed. The apples were picked and stored. Potatoes lay in their bins in the cellar. Crocks of applebutter and cans of molasses sat in the washhouse loft. Sauerkraut stood fermenting in its stone jar. Dried beans tied tightly in cloth pokes awaited consumption. Other foods had been preserved and dried. Feed for stock filled the corn crib and the mows in the barn. The wood for fuel was cut and lay in a big heap ready for burning. The heating stoves had been installed in the front room and parlor. And the school bell rang each morning, telling the community it was "going back to school time."

I was no longer a little girl creating havoc with a pair of scissors and certain parts of her outfit, but a third-year scholar traversing the road to this school each day with my brothers and sisters and friends.

Little did we anticipate the events that were to follow —one event that would lead to hardships, suffering, and tragedy for our family and community; another, something of a phenomenon of nature that propelled us into a topsy-turvy world.

Fall was changing gradually into winter and the wind was gusty and chilly as we walked briskly down the road in the four o'clock sun-time. "We" were my brothers and sisters and I, and our friends, the Bowmans and Frances Diehl.

35

Elizabeth, addressing me, asked, "I like those songs we are practicing for Patrons' Meeting, don't you?"

"Yes, especially 'Poor Old Maids.'* I might say a recitation, too; that's what teacher said today."

"We didn't have much of any lessons this afternoon on account of practicing. That was fun!" Wilbur added.

Frances D. laughed. "It sure musta' been for you and Virgil the way you all were gigglin' behind the organ. What were you doing back there?"

"None of your business, Frances Diehl! Yeah, and how about what happened to you today?"

"What happened to you, Frances?" asked Ruth.

Frances, who was funny and jolly and enjoyed a joke, even when it was on herself, proceeded to tell us what happened. "This morning before school took up, I was playing out by the coal house. Well, I found one of the shingles they had pulled off the roof when they put on the new tar paper, and took it in to the teacher. I told her she could use it for a paddle today if she needed it for someone bad. I didn't expect her to use it on me, but she sure did. That's the last time I'll try to be helpful to her."

Bertha joked, "Frances, how did it feel to get your backsides shingled?"

We were still laughing when we reached our crossroads and went our separate ways.

When we walked in, Mother was ready with her list of chores: "Children, get your clothes changed and let's get our work done. It gets dark early these evenings. Wilbur, I think Pappy has a job for you at the barn. Jake, you and Mary get at your milking right away. Esther, get the basket and gather the eggs, and then you and Frances can pick up some cobs and chips to start the fires in the morning. After that, each of you bring in a load of wood. Ruth will help me get supper on the table."

We all hurried into our everyday clothes and scattered into many directions over the farm. I took the egg basket and went to the nests that were located in the barn, sheds,

---

*Glossary

36

and corn crib, and collected the eggs I found there; then I moved to the chickenhouse and very carefully laid those in the basket, too. Eggs were important to us as they were exchanged for some of the necessities the farm could not produce. While I gathered eggs from one nest, a hen in the adjoining nest stood up with a "Ku-ku-ku-kudeckut," notifying me that she had just laid her egg. "Old Biddy, you are pretty late with that today, aren't you?"

As she moved away, I put her egg in the basket on top of the others. A rooster nearby began fussing and tried to flop me; perhaps thinking I had stolen his unhatched baby.

"Shoo! Shoo! Get away, you! Shoo! Shoo!" I shouted, kicking at the pesky bird and trying to protect my basket of eggs all at the same time. Finally, I made it to the door, closing him in with his harem.

As I set the egg basket down, I called to Frances, "Bring the bucket and let's go get our chips."

We searched around the woodpile and the place where Jasper had been chopping wood until we had filled our bucket. As Frances carried it into the kitchen and deposited it by the stove, I filled my arms with wood and unloaded it in the woodbox that sat behind the stove. When Frances returned with her load a few minutes later, Mother remarked, "That's a mighty small armful, Frances."

Without comment, Frances left the kitchen for the front room where I joined her to warm my hands by the black stove with its tall pipe that extended up through the ceiling into the room above and elbowed over to the chimney, conducting the smoke away, and at the same time, adding warmth to the room.

That night after supper, we sat around the dining room table with our books spread out in front of us and a pan of apples in the middle, as we studied by lamplight. There was no assumption that apples were brain food, but there is one conclusion that could be reached—in the quantities we ate, they were a good cathartic when one lacked an abundance of green things and a variety of fresh fruits in his diet. As we munched and studied, we got into a few battles, as we did frequently.

37

With my reader in front of me, I droned out a little poem which I was memorizing for Patrons' Meeting:

> At evening when I go to bed,
> I see the stars shine overhead;
> They are the little—

"Moth-er! Esther is studying out loud, and that be-fuddles me," Ruth called.

"Esther, come on in here and say your poem to me so you won't bother the others," said Mother, attempting to quiet things.

As I sat in front of Mother, I began once more:

Daisies

> At evening when I go to bed,
> I see the stars shine overhead;
> They are the little daisies white
> That dot the meadows of the night.

> And often, while I'm dreaming so,
> Across the sky the moon will go;
> It is a lady, sweet and fair
> Who comes to gather daisies there.

> For when at morning I arise,
> There's not a star left in the skies;
> She's picked them all and dropped them down
> Into the meadows of the town.*

Mary cried disgustedly, "Now Wilbur is reading out loud! Moth-er!"

This time Pappy took over, "Wilbur, come and recite to me. I'd like to hear what you have learned."

Wilbur stood up straight in front of Pappy, sort of threw his chest out and began reciting without a book in a loud sonorous voice:

---

*Graded Classics Second Reader, B. F. Johnson Publishing Company, Richmond, Virginia, 1902.

Napoleon was sitting in his tent and before him—"*

In the dining room, studying went on quietly and uninterrupted for a period.

Finally, "Mother, Jake has gone to sleep."

Mother said in response, "It's about time for all of you to put your books away and go to bed. Be sure to outen' your lights before you go."

December came, and with it the weather turned bleak and cold. The cows and horses huddled together in the barnyard against the strawrick or in the slanting rays of the winter sun. The chickens were reluctant to venture even their beaks out of their houses. The condensation on the walls and windows of our house trickled down in little rivulets, and in the morning when we arose it was frozen on the windows in beautiful patterns—ferns, forests, and tall grasses. Well bundled up, we hurried about our tasks with more alacrity. And at night the homemade covers were piled high over us as we slept in our unheated bedrooms.

One evening in early December, a buttermilk sky indicated that we would have snow. The next morning we arose to a white world—unblemished whiteness, no chimneys belching soot, no cars with their black exhaust to mar its pure beauty.

As we were busily preparing to perform the morning chores, the telephone jingled two longs and one short. On the other end, Margaret relayed a message to us. "Father is going to take us all to school this morning in the big sleigh; he said for you to meet us at the crossroads about eight-thirty."

The sleigh to which she referred was the most wonderful vehicle man ever fashioned. Cousin Otis had forged the wide iron bands from two large wagon wheels into sled runners. He then constructed a frame to which these runners were attached. To complete the job, his farm

---

*Glossary

wagon was robbed of the eight or ten foot body which was secured to the chassis. The neighborhood now had a marvelous two-horse sleigh.

It is impossible to imagine a more delightful ride with one's friends. On those days the distance to school seemed all too short; contrary to the way we usually felt. So with lunch buckets in hand and book satchels flung across our shoulders, we exceeded the speed limit as we dashed to the crossroads. We buried our feet and legs in the straw that had been provided, and settled down for a merry ride and exciting chatter.

Two evenings later while the snow still blanketed the ground, we all readied ourselves to go to school in that same sleigh. The program on which we had been working diligently was to be presented at the Patrons' Meeting. As we entered the schoolhouse the fires were roaring in the potbellied stoves, for they had been well stoked against the cold night. The blackboard between the two rooms had been lifted and pinned to the ceiling; and a stage had been built in one end to make an auditorium of sorts. Mothers and fathers and small brothers and sisters were squeezed into the same desks that we children occupied every day. In the stage area and in the hall leading to it, where all the performers were assembled, excitement reigned; but finally the show was about to begin as families awaited expectantly. There was no awareness of any potential for disaster that this assemblage might precipitate in the community. The performance began with the smallest ones, which included my sister Frances; they made their entrance with a drill called "The Sunflowers." Each child carried a huge crepe paper flower and executed certain formations to the organ playing of Miss Alice, the primary teacher. They concluded this first part with singing. At the close of each child's participation, he would return to sit with parents while the program proceeded.

My room, consisting of two classes as did all, filed onto the stage and stood in two straight rows for our songs. Our first selection was, "We've Got the Mumps,"* which we performed with jaws puffed out and bound with

*Glossary

40

handkerchiefs knotted on top of our heads; then followed, "Twenty Years Ago."* Next I stepped to the front and said my well rehearsed "Daisies." For our last number, we donned sunbonnets and sang, "Poor Old Maids." The audience expressed their appreciation with their clapping and laughter.

Jake's class gave a dialogue, "The Train Ride," in which Jake thundered out his own line with about as much expression as a cigar store Indian, "A-man-had-his-eye-on-a-seat-and-a-woman-came-in-and-sat-on-it."

By the time Wilbur's class had sung, "Carve that possum, carve that possum, Hee! Hee! Hee!"* with Wilbur's monotone voice bellowing out the final line, "And I'll 'low you all the tail and the ha'r," the room was rocking with laughter. As the crescendo of pleasure and laughter rose, so, too, did the heat produced by the almost red hot stoves and the human generators crowded into the space provided by two classrooms. Faces were ruddy with heat and health, and those bodies nearest the stove were perspiring profusely.

As the program proceeded apace, the climax came with Bertha's recital of "The Raven" by Edgar Allan Poe. She stood on the stage with supreme confidence in the knowledge that she had mastered this long poem completely. I had little concept of the meaning of:

'Take thy beak from out my heart, and take thy form
    from off my door!
Quoth the raven, 'Nevermore.'

Yet it all sounded so beautiful as she recited it with deep feeling. I shared in a small way the pride that shone on my Pappy's and Mother's faces and in their eyes as she concluded her piece.

While the curtain was slowly and laboriously lowered on the final performance, friends and neighbors mingled and chatted for a few minutes, expressing their pride in their

---

*Glossary

own children and complimenting others. Perhaps also, they wanted to linger a bit longer to absorb the warmth of the room before they faced the frosty, cold, night air. As we mingled and commingled in the hot unventilated room, we were unsuspecting of any problems these actions would create. But within a very few days thereafter, the influenza began spreading through the community with octopus-like tentacles, snatching up families one by one, often attacking many members in one family simultaneously. Our family did not escape; and now it included Charlie, who had returned home at war's end, and Elizabeth, whose school had been closed because of the epidemic in that community.

One by one and two by two we took to our beds as our temperatures shot up and we were miserable with aches and pains. Finally, our upstairs was like an infirmary with beds completely filled with patients. At length, the only ones left unattacked by the bug were Pappy, Mother, and Mary who ministered to us and took care of the work. They looked after the stock; did the milking and all the outdoor chores; kept the fires going; carried food and medicine upstairs to the sick. Often Mary growled and complained about how hard she had to work, and because she constantly had to carry out potties. We had no pine-scented fresheners in those days; so after each elimination, Mother burned a string which was supposed to remove the bad odors. I don't profess to be knowledgeable enough to know the scientific principle involved in this, if any. Uncle Charlie gave instructions on proper care to the best of his knowledge. His prescription was to take aspirin for the aches and pains and salts to keep the bowels open.

Uncle Charlie Harshbarger was Mother's brother and the community doctor; community in this concept was a very broad one and stretched for many miles. His office was the countryside over which he traveled. Uncle Charlie was the embodiment of the country physician which today many wistfully remember. He was the guardian of our family health from delivery to adulthood.

However, the winter of 1918–1919 was the time of the

first great flu epidemic in this country; and doctors were unprepared to cope with the situation. Very few families, if any, were left unaffected. Many times when all members were sick simultaneously and they attempted to care for each other, pneumonia and death would result. Neighbor helped neighbor whenever possible, but this was quite often difficult.

The marvel of it all for the Pence family was that Mother and Pappy and one daughter were able to keep well so that they could care for all the rest. Somewhere in God's great plan for life, it must have been our destiny to grow into adulthood, to accomplish the purpose for which we were created. That was God's little miracle for us.

Just as earlier we took to bed, so in the ensuing days we left them one by one and two by two—pale, weak, and ravenous—but at length we all weathered it. Since schools and churches had been closed because of the epidemic, the next days gave us time for recuperation and relaxation: we played indoor games, we read books, our older sisters cut quilt squares and sewed them, and we younger children were obstreperous and crabbid.

As Mother, Elizabeth, Bertha, Ruth, and Mary sat sewing, Elizabeth suggested, "Esther, get a thimble and you all can play 'Monkey in Sight.'"

While I went to the sewing machine drawer for a thimble, Wilbur shouted, "I wanta' be it first!" and he ran from the room.

I hid the thimble in Mother's lap and called, "Monkey in Sight!"

Wilbur reappeared and began the search, alternately going from hot to cold, until finally, he shouted as he spied the thimble in Mother's lap, "Monkey in Sight!"

For a time, we youngsters went round and round in turns, hiding the thimble in all the unusual or difficult places we could think up, aided by our mother and sisters, but making sure it was partly in view.

Frances, on one of her turns, accused, "You hid it too hard! I can't find it! The monkey is not in sight! Why did you do that?"

Jake said, "Look out the window, Frances. Maybe the monkey is swinging by his tail in a tree."

Frances, who was ever unsuspicious, ran to the window, "I don't see no monkey."

Mother quipped, "The only monkeys around here are the ones in this room."

By now, having decided it was time to conclude "Monkey in Sight," she added, "Why don't you play 'Fist-Off?' "

"I'd like to play that if Wilbur and Jake don't get too rough," I agreed.

"We won't, we won't!"

So we began stacking our fists with thumbs up, each grasping the one below it.

Mary, who by now was tired of stitching together quilt squares volunteered, "I'll be your leader."

To Frances, whose fist was on top, she asked, "Take it off, or knock it off?"

"Take it off," Frances said, as she jerked her fist away.

Next to Wilbur, "Take it off, or knock it off?"

Wilbur challenged, "Knock it off!"

Mary, as she attempted to do so, cried, "Your old hard fist hurts my hand!"

"And you are hurting my thumb by squeezing it so hard!" I complained.

Wilbur finally acceded to our complaints and removed his fist. The game proceeded apace, as Mary continued the question, "Take it off, or knock it off?" and the responses were either one or the other until she reached my fist on the bottom.

Pointing to it she asked, "What's that?"

My response, "Bread and cheese."

"Where's my part?"

"I put it on a window and a little black dog got it."

"Where's the dog?"

"In the woods, dead."

"Where's the woods?"

"The fire burned it."

"Where's the fire?"

"The water outened it."

"Where's the water?"

"The ox drank it."

"Where's the ox?"

"Butcher killed it."

"Where's the butcher?"

"Rope hung him."

"Where's the rope?"

"Rats gnawed it."

"Where's the rats?"

"The cats caught them."

"Where's the cats?"

"Behind the church door cracking hickory nuts, first one shows his teeth gets a big slap in his mouth."

Our efforts were then turned to inducing each other to laugh and show his teeth, and to resist doing so ourselves. But the act of slapping anyone's mouth was more bluff than real.

Through the entire course of our game, Mary had been vigorously chewing on a wad of gum.

Wilbur, who could no longer suppress his craving, asked, "Mary, where did you get that chewing gum? Why don't you give us some?"

Mary said, "None of your bizness. I didn't have very much and you don't give any to me when you have some. It's all anyway."

Then began the refrain that we always hurled at each other at such times:

> Chaw, chaw, chaw with all your might,
> Chaw, chaw, not a second losing,
> Chaw, chaw, chaw from morn till night.
> Put it on the bedpost,
> Leave it there while snoozing.
> Chaw, chaw, chaw with all your heart,
> Chaw, chaw, not a second losing.
> Chaw, chaw, naught but death can part
> Mary and her chewing gum.

Whether this gem came down to us from a former generation, or whether it came from the fertile combined brains of the Pence tribe, has never been answered. Who gets the credit makes little difference, for it certainly is no masterpiece as a lyric or melody. The singsong chant which we used could hardly be rated as a melody.

Later that evening when the men came in from their evening chores, Pappy observed, "The sky looks like snow and the air feels like snow. We'll have snow on top of snow the way it appears now."

Once again Pappy was right, for just at dusk it began, at first large flakes, popcorn flakes, but as dark settled upon us it came down fine and fast, portending a big snowfall.

After supper was eaten and we had cleaned up the dishes we sat in the front room with our nightly pan of apples, trying to decide on a game to play before bedtime.

Mother, interrupting our thoughts, ordered, "Esther, you and Bertha cover my flowers before it gets so late; it's so cold they might freeze tonight."

Bertha collected several newspapers, and we went to the kitchen where Mother's stair-step flower stand stood in the end of the room away from the stove and by the window. It held a motley, rather scraggly array of plants —geraniums, cacti, begonias, and unnamed varieties. It's to be admitted that when it came to raising house plants, Mother didn't exactly have a green thumb. There must have been many other things of greater importance to her; this was not one of her first priorities. However, a flower stand seemed to be a part of every household; so we carefully placed newspapers between the plants and the window, draping others down over the plants to protect them. Having completed our task to Bertha's satisfaction, we rejoined the others in the living room where a game of "Who You Are? Where You Are? and Whatcha' Doing?" was already in progress.

As our interest in play fizzled out, we were still reluctant to leave the warmth of the front room for our bedrooms upstairs. I quickly suggested, "Mother, tell us 'Miss Bets.'"

And Mother, who was aware of the importance of sending her big family to bed happy, began the old story whose origin we never knew, but to which we never tired of listening. First, she pulled both lips back over her teeth, which added to the humor of the story, for it gave her voice an unusual sound and pitch; and thus she began:

Bets and I were girls together. Bets was married and I wasn't. One day I was a sittin' and a knittin' and a sewin', when I heard a rap at my door. I went to the door, and lo-and-behold, it was Bets. I said, 'Bets, won't you come in?' And she did. I asked her how many children she had and she said she had twelve. One had green hair and yellow eyes, one had striped hair and speckled eyes, one had stringy hair and a turned up nose, and one had purple hair and checkered eyes and she was the prettiest; but she had died. I asked, 'Bets, are you hungry?' And she said she was. I took her to my cellar and she ate all my potatoes, she ate all my pickles, and all my cabbage, and all my beans. Law, but Bets did eat! 'Bets, what kind of a horse are you driving, bay or sorrel?' And she said she did. And I asked her which way the horse wagged its tail, toward the rising or the setting of the sun, and she said it did. And it all passed away in a speeter's web.

Mouth back to normal, she said, "Now it's time for all of you to get to bed before *you* pass away into a speeter's web."

Mother and others of her generation could have furnished competition to Dr. Seuss in spinning fanciful stories for the amusement of children.

That night with comforts piled high over us, we were glad we slept double, for we served as heat generators to each other. I was happy to have Frances as a bedfellow in winter, for she radiated warmth like a heating stove.

We slept on unaware of nature's phenomenal performance outside. It continued to snow, until finally as

47

morning neared, we awoke—not to the silence of snow, but to the sound of sleet and rain rat-a-tat-tat-ing on our tin roof, freezing and clinging to everything it touched. By midmorning it was all over; the sun came out and beheld a white, wild, topsy-turvy world! Everything was encrusted with a thick frozen coat of ice, sleet, and snow.

When Pappy, Jasper, and Charlie came in from the barn, Pappy said, "You children won't believe what it is like out; I don't think I'll tell, but I'll let you experience it for yourselves."

That speech was enough incentive for us, and we quickly followed Mother's instructions to bundle up well. We almost tumbled pell-mell over one another as we hurried outdoors.

How deep the snow was! Surely we couldn't walk in it! We would sink in up to our knees and beyond! We gingerly stepped upon it; and to our absolute wonderment, we did not sink in at all! We were astounded as we tested our feet; astronauts on a white untried moon world! Confidence came upon walking about. Finally, we stomped, we jumped up and down, we ran; there seemed to be no way of breaking in the thick crust of sleet and ice that had formed over the snow. We chased each other. We tried to skate; mostly we slid around on our backsides. We stepped over the yard fence with ease. The world was our toy, our playground, our winter wonderland! We knew precisely what we were going to do as soon as dinner was over.

After cleaning up the table and washing dishes, we assembled our equipment: boards, pieces of linoleum, an old dish pan, a large long-handled scoop, our old homemade sled; and worked our way up the steep slope of the barn hill. This took a little doing, as we had no ski lifts and very little foothold in the hard frozen sleet that covered everywhere. Nature surely had never provided a better surface for coasting. We climbed in or on our makeshift toboggans and down the hill we sped—across the lot, out the road gate, and down the big road a distance before we came to a halt. It was unqualified ecstasy!

"Here I come! Whoopee!"

The boys were riding flat on their tummies or on their backs with feet straight up in the air.

"Get out of my way, Frances, I'm coming!"

"I never had so much fun coasting!"

"Watch me, Bertha!"

"Gee, I about busted myself when I fell that time!"

"Let's two of us try to get on this piece of linoleum!" The situation invited experimentation.

By this time, Charlie and Jasper were intrigued, and had decided to join in the sport.

Ruth running back to the house, shouted, "Mother! Pappy! Elizabeth! Come and see us coast!"

Throwing wraps over their shoulders and heads, they came to the dining room porch and watched the uninhibited merriment of our performance.

"Watch this, Mother! I'm the only one who can do this!"

"Look, Pappy! Look at me!"

They stood enjoying our antics with an occasional word of caution, "Be careful now, don't get too wild, boys! Watch out for Frances and Esther!"

Frances, who was on her backsides more than her feet, was laughing and grunting, "Wupsy! Wupsy! Wupsy!" with each spill.

And thus we stayed on until exhaustion time.

At night the whole community of children, and sometimes adults, gathered for coasting parties at some agreed upon hill, not always the same one. We made a big bonfire at the top to warm our fingers, toes, faces, and backsides in between rides. We felt that not even one flake of this snow should be wasted. Amazingly enough, the temperature continued quite cold and the crust remained until the school was called back into session after the flu epidemic had subsided. But now, even walking to school was fun, for we could take crosscuts through the fields and meadows, walking on top of the snow and stepping across fences as we went. Such an unusual snow truly provided us with very real, but very incredible experiences, and we made the most of it.

This winter of 1918–1919 is still so vivid in our memories; one that we recall with both pain and pleasure.

Chapter 4

EASTER EGGS

Long before the terms ecology and conservation became public bywords, the farmer was "at one" with nature. Experience had taught him that the universe around him and his relation to it were the substance of life itself. His experiences were poignant and very real. He knew about nature's balance, about life cycles and time cycles, about sowing and reaping. He had learned about the conservation of nature's bounties, about returning elements to the soil and having it come back to him, sometimes a hundredfold. He knew about the weather, its changes and its foibles, and how it related to the sustenance of life for his family. The eternal order of the seasons had taught him that there is a time for all things: planting and tending; harvesting and resting.

Springtime on the farm was beautiful, and its advent was greeted with admiration, joy, and expectation. For all the Pence brood, it was the bursting forth from the chrysalis in which we had been encased all winter. Even our actions and our constant chatter seemed to take on new life from the warm sunshine, the fragrant woods and meadows, and the wonderfully fresh and invigorating spring breezes.

School was out for the day, but no yellow school bus was at the door to give us a ride home; so down the dusty road we came on legs accustomed to walking the two miles to and from school, all twelve of our group:

Margaret, Elizabeth, Virginia, and Carl—the Bowmans; Frances Diehl; and the Pences—Bertha, Ruth, Mary, Wilbur, Jacob, Esther, and Frances. On this day we were in no hurry; we knew we would arrive home in time to get our evening chores done before dark, for it was spring and the days were growing longer. We wanted to enjoy the minutes outdoors as long as possible, so we just ambled along at an easy gait—the boys occasionally kicking the dust or clods with the toes of their almost-worn out shoes, the girls pairing off in little groups with their favorite friends. For me, that meant my pal Elizabeth Bowman, who was my soulmate over the years and with whom I shared many inspired activities—sometimes productive and sometimes not so productive. We made chitchat about our personal interests and the happenings of the day at school. There were no televisions and radios to broaden our horizons or perspectives, but nevertheless, it must be admitted that our imaginations ran rather rampant at times.

Frances D. laughed. "I want to tell you something funny. Today Wilbur and Virgil (our cousin) were hoppin' up and down in the aisle between the desks, makin' out like rabbits, and teacher caught them. You know what she did, she made them keep on hoppin'. They really got tired before she let them stop. I reckon they won't be long-eared bunnies anyways soon again."

"I'm going to tell Pappy and Mother on you, Wilbur, for worrying the teacher like that," Mary threatened.

Wilbur retorted, "You hush up, you old blabber mouth, Mary, and you, too, Frances Diehl, or I'll tell on you all having to stand in the corner for talking! I'll tell your grandma on you, Frances!"

In the meantime, Elizabeth and I were holding our own little private conversation.

Elizabeth said, "I had fun at recess time today, didn't you?"

"Yeah, I liked that game, 'King William,' didn't you?"

"I sure did. Were you chosen by any one?"

"One time David Long chose me. He's my favorite boy," I giggled.

51

"I wish he had chosen me. I like him, too, but that old Tommy Crowe chose me. I hate him!"

"Yeah, me, too! Today he called me 'A Dumb Dutchman'! He's so snobby. I can't help it if I'm Dutch," I replied disgustedly.

"He called me that, too, but we're just as good as he is."

"You know what I wish? I wish I lived in East Virginia. In history class today, we had a lesson called Ante-Bellum Days, and it told all about the big houses with tall white pillars in front in which they lived. And they had slaves to wait on them and do all the work. They didn't have all these hard jobs to do like we have. And gee, the way those girls dressed in lacy gowns with great, long, full skirts, and seven petticoats, and ribbons in their hair, and button shoes on their feet—they must have been beautiful! And they had dances, where they danced until twelve o'clock with their boyfriends—the book said these dances were called 'balls.' "

"Balls! Balls! That's funny, how could they be called balls? Balls are what we play with," argued Elizabeth.

"Well, that's what it said. I sure would like to have one of those dresses and some button shoes. I'd like to learn to dance, too."

"What good would it do ya' to learn to dance? We don't have any dances around here. Your parents wouldn't let ya' dance anyway. I don't think I'd like to wear seven petticoats. Esther, I like the song 'King William' that we sang in the game we played today; let's sing it again."

King William

> King William was King James's son,
> All the royal race he won.
> Upon his breast he wore a star
> That was called the life of war.
> Go choose your east,
> Go choose your west,
> Go choose the one that you love best.

If she's not here to take her part,
Choose the next one to your heart.
Down upon this carpet, you must kneel,
Sure's the grass grows in the field.
Salute your bride and kiss her sweet.
Rise again upon your feet.*

By the time we reached our crossroads and were ready to tarry awhile under our favorite tree, everyone had joined in and the lyrics had been sung and resung.

Bertha, turning to her brothers and sisters, said, "I reckon we'd better be gettin' home. I got some studyin' to do tonight, so I must get my work done."

"So have I. The teacher gave us a lota' 'rithmetic problems to do, and they are those old hard carpeting problems," added Ruth.

Mary, who was not anxious to get home to her work, said, "Frances D. and I have some secrets to talk about first; I'll be along in a minute."

"Come on Wilbur and Jake, and Esther and Frances," said Bertha, taking over.

As we walked in the gate, we were greeted by clusters of spring blooms along the three sides of a white paling fence. Mother's Easter flowers, which had been blossoming a few each day, seemed to have responded suddenly to the day's warm sunshine, all opening their petals and nodding their heads in the breeze, saying, "Hi! Look at us!" There were the buttercups, the narcissus, the crocus, the snow drops, the butter and eggs, and the blue hyacinths in great profusion.

Bertha, thinking out loud, said, "Hey, that reminds me that Easter is not much over a week away. It's time to hide eggs. Are you ready, Ruth?"

At the supper table we continued to discuss this subject, and got Mother's and Pappy's consent to start hiding anytime, but with this warning from Mother, "Now don't you children bother any of my settin' hens and try to take their eggs. I have several on their nests already."

---

*Glossary

"Who'd want to mess with any old settin' hens? They'd pick your fingers off!" retorted Jake.

Mary, as she had threatened, started tattling, "Wilbur got in trouble at school today. He and Virgil were hoppin' like rabbits up and down the aisles between the desks, and the teacher made them keep hoppin.' I guess they thought they were Easter Bunnies."

"Show us your tail, Wilbur. I wanta' see your tail," laughed Charlie.

Bertha, adding her bit, "Yeah, Wilbur, flop your big long ears, too."

Pappy admonished, "Now, Wilbur, and all of you listen to me. I have talked to you so many times about the importance of getting all the education you can. The world is changing so fast and there is so much for you to learn. Now let's stop worrying our teachers and get down to business, or I'll have to take you in hand. Do you understand, Wilbur, and the rest of you, too?"

"Yes, sir."

"Yes, sir."

"Yes, sir, yes, sir," we all said, not wanting Pappy to take us in hand, knowing that sometimes this could be rather painful.

"Today at recess time Tommy Crowe called me 'A Dumb Dutchman.' I don't like being called that!" I said, changing the subject.

Mother smiled, knowing that Tommy himself was of Dutch parentage, as were most of the inhabitants of our area. So she counseled me, "Esther, pay no attention to that kind of talk; you are not dumb and you should be proud of your Dutch background. Your ancestors were fine people who lived in Germany many years ago, and came to this country so that they could be free to worship as they pleased."

And Pappy added, "Yes, Esther, they were honest upright people of whom it has often been said, 'Their word is as good as their bond.' "

"What does that mean, Pappy?"

"It means that they tried to be truthful at all times, and if they made a promise, they really meant it."

54

I understood what they were trying to say to me; but I still wasn't quite sure that I wouldn't hit Tommy, or anyone else, who ever called me "A Dumb Dutchman" again.

The next days preceding Easter were full of activity on our farm, with scurrying hither and thither from the hen house to the barn, to the corncrib, to the buggy shed. We never confined our hens to the chickenhouse; they were allowed to roam about, finding nests in boxes, barrels, buckets, haymows—anywhere they discovered grass or straw enough for nesting purposes. So as we sneaked eggs from these nests, we were being very cautious and mysterious, sometimes rather clumsily so, no doubt. All the while, we were surreptitiously spying on others, for it was an allowable part of the game to confiscate another's eggs. It added much to one's sense of accomplishment, if he could raid another's hiding place, but usually brought disappointment to the raidee. Many times through the week, we would find that all our eggs we had so carefully gathered and concealed in what we thought was a Jim Dandy hiding place, had disappeared. Then we would have to find another cache and start over again. The bane of all our efforts were the clandestine operations of Bertha and Ruth. These two often pooled their devious maneuvers, dividing the eggs they cooperatively confiscated from the rest of us. Between the two of them, they had a real spy network going. The C.I.A., in not hiring those two, overlooked the best sleuths in the business. Our juvenile efforts couldn't possibly cope very successfully with their operation. And Mother and Pappy rarely interfered with our little disputes and petty quarrels. Their unspoken philosophy was to let us take our lumps and fend for ourselves; thereby becoming stronger human beings more competent to cope with the world of our future. They foresaw this to be a very different world from their own present one.

Other activities were taking place this week. Mother had us fetch a half gallon can of beet pickles from the cellar, and had poured them over about two dozen hard boiled eggs in a crock. What could be more delicious than pickled eggs—or more colorful? I have often wondered why we didn't have them more often throughout the year, since we all enjoyed them so much. If you have never had the pleasure of eating these, try them sometime. They also make a very attractive hors-d'oeuvre on any modern table. Near the latter part of the week, Mother had cooked half of a large sugar-cured ham to be sliced and eaten with our eggs on Easter Sunday. Sugar curing was the Dutch way of processing hams, and I maintain it is still the best meat cure.

Throughout the week, I would hide eggs one day, only to have them disappear by the next. Judging from some of the other doleful expressions, their success must have been as limited. We never quite knew whether Bertha and Ruth might be the culprits, or whether it might be Pappy, who was a pretty good sleuth himself. On Good Friday, I finally found a hiding place that I felt would certainly be secure from the eyes of other snoopers if I were very careful. A wooden nail keg sat in the corner of the barn about two thirds full of hay and straw, and had provided a very good nest for some hen. I very meticulously removed some of the nesting material and then placed my eggs on the remainder; and then as meticulously, I placed the hay back on top of my eggs, smoothing it out and trying to camouflage it to appear as before. Cautiously peeping out the barn door, I made sure no one was watching and very innocently strolled to the house.

Friday passed; I was safe—Saturday passed, and I was still safe—until late evening when in came Pappy with a hat full of eggs. My heart went pitapat. Where had he gotten them? Were they mine? The suspense was not long—the answer was forthcoming. He had discovered my secret place and also Wilbur's. It made it a bit easier to have company in my misery. From the looks of the others, there wouldn't be many of us who had successfully kept our hiding places secret; even Ruth's eggs had been absconded by someone, she had admitted earlier. Bertha continued to look smug and happy over what

56

she apparently considered a very profitable week, which would end in total success in the morning.

On Easter Sunday we were all arising when dawn blinked at us through our farmhouse windows. There were very few "sleeping lates" on our farm even on the Sabbath. For there were chores to perform and breakfast to be eaten before the surrey and buggy were hitched up and everyone was dressed and ready to go, but we were our own efficiency experts. We felt it important to be at church on time, our plain white church that served this community of people known as The Brethren, formerly called Dunkers. By the time we had assembled in the kitchen area to disperse to our various chores, including the bringing in of eggs (if you were lucky enough to still have a cache) our tall Pappy appeared in the door with a merry twinkle in his blue eyes and a basket in one hand. The basket contained a mound of brownish hen eggs.

"I found these eggs at the foot of the ladder to the haymow, down under the hay," he said.

All eyes turned in one direction—toward Bertha—for there was little doubt as to whom they belonged. From our usually effervescent one, the silence was deafening. The smugness was replaced by the most crestfallen and dejected look—she was completely shorn of her glory. The mirth in Pappy's face, which burst out loud, became a mighty chorus; for while we might have empathized a bit with her in her chagrin, we all felt that she had at last gotten her come-uppance. However, any feelings that may have been expressed or felt at that moment were soon lost in the business of the morning, and besides, we all had accepted at its earliest initiation that this was a fun activity, so the disappointments never went too deep. Mother and Pappy always said, "It's not whether you win or lose, it's how you play the game."

I have concluded by this time, that Pappy had something going between him and those hens, inasmuch as he usually knew where all the eggs were. Could hens be participants in E.S.P.?

Mother laughing, said, "These eggs will certainly make

a nice plateful for dinner. Bertha, do you like fried eggs?"

With that, we all went separate ways to our individual morning chores.

Easter dinner was special! The menu was eggs!

Since most farmers produced many eggs, it may seem surprising today that eating all the eggs they wanted was such a treat to farm people. The truth is that there were generally very few of them eaten; they were sold or traded for necessary items that had to be purchased from the store. So it was a treat for us to see our table spread with a large plate of fried eggs, one vegetable dish filled with soft boiled eggs, and another with pickled eggs that were now bright red and well saturated with the flavor of spiced beets. The crowning glory was a plate of beautiful, pink, sliced, sugar-cured ham.

Wilbur, whose appraisal of his appetite surpassed the capacity of his stomach, asked, "How many eggs can you eat, Jake?"

"I can eat more'n you," Jake bragged.

"How many?"

"I can eat five."

"I can eat six."

"I can eat eight."

"I can eat ten times more'n you can eat."

Ruth giggled. "If you boys eat that many, you'll be saying cluck cluck and layin' eggs before the day is over."

Pappy, who began to think the humor was getting over-done, interrupted, "That will do, children. Let's eat your dinners now."

There wasn't much urging necessary to get compliance with that order, and though not in the astronomical numbers Wilbur was boasting about, we began making away with great quantities of eggs.

Pappy, turning to serious thoughts, said, "Brother Early preached a powerful sermon on the resurrection this morning."

"I thought so, too; he made it plain enough for even the children to understand," replied Mother.

Wilbur asked, "Why did Brother Long have to pray and pray and pray? I watched the big clock and he prayed for more than fifteen minutes!"

"My knees got so tired and Frances went to sleep. I had to punch her to wake her up at the Amen," I added.

Mary, interrupting the serious conversation, said, "The Bowmans and Frances D. said they could come over to play this afternoon."

Bertha immediately suggested, "Let's get cleaned up so we can play when they get here," and she began clearing the table.

When eleven people move with one accord, scraping chairs as they push back from the table and crawling across benches with "lubbardy" feet, the din is thunderous. This was so usual at our house that it passed unnoticed, at least no nerves screamed in response. To mention the neighbor children's coming was to get the table cleared and dishes washed in a hurry.

When our friends arrived, we moved outdoors with one unspoken accord. No one had to ask where we would play on such a beautiful day.

Ruth suggested, "Let's play 'Hidey Who' (Hide and Go-seek), then the little ones can play too."

"Let's set our limits first," added Mary.

Wilbur volunteered, "All right, I'll do that. We can hide in the barn, under the barn bridge, in the machine shed, in the buggy shed, and around the woodpile; but you can't go to the house, or yard, the chickenhouses, and the fields. Everyone understand that?"

"Yes, yes!"

"Yes!"

"Let's play!"

Frances D., anxious, too, about getting started, said, "I'll count out to see who is it."

And she began,

Eerie Eirie, Acrie Ann, Phyllis Phyollis,
Nichris John, Kribley Krobley, Vergie Marey,
Singum, Sangum, Borney Buck!*

---

*Origin unknown

"Margaret, you're it."

As Margaret plastered her face against the barn door (our base) and counted, we took off in all possible directions and more. The smaller ones of the group, Ruth and Ruby B., were taken in tow by Bertha and Frances D. My bosom pal, Elizabeth, and I charged off to the barn together, our roving eyes giving it the "once over" for the perfect hiding place. We found it! On either side of us, there were great upright timbers which were a part of the framework that supported the barn. Nailed on to these were walls approximately thirty inches high to form the mows on each side which were the repositories for the hay and the wheat sheaves, after they were hauled in from the fields. There was just enough space behind the hay and between the timbers for little bodies to slide into; so we slid, completely hidden from view.

Our own voices never raising above a whisper, we heard the thwacking on the barn door and:

"One two three for Mary!"

"Free, free, one two three for me!"

"One two three for Ruth and Ruby!"

"One two three for Jake!"

And on and on it seemed for an interminable length of time.

"I wish they would give us up; this hay is sticking me," I said with a sigh.

"Me too, and it's hot in here," added Elizabeth.

Finally, from outside came, "Where are Esther and Elizabeth?"

Then, "We give up! Come on home free!"

Glad to oblige, we wriggled, and pulled, and pushed ourselves out of our slots.

Elizabeth, sniffing, "Phe-e-ew-w! I smell something awful stinken!"

"I smell it, too. What is it?"

"Esther! Look at your new sweater!"

I looked. I smelled. And what I beheld and smelled was awful! On the front of my brand-new red sweater was a great smear of black chicken manure; the job could not have been more complete had it been done deliberately.

Apparently, some chicken had been there ahead of me, and since chickens are not particularly concerned about the location of their toilet facilities, it had freely used this spot. After that experience, if I had expressed my thoughts on chicken manure, I would have done it thusly:

Chicken Manure

Chicken manure is of two kinds. One kind is whitish and grayish in color, kinda' mingled. It don't smell so bad, just sort of middlin' bad. The other kind is black and puddin'y looking and its smells terrible, and that's all I know about chicken manure, and that's enough.

Needless to say, I had to leave the game and dash to the house immediately, leaving the laughter of the group behind. After scraping off the excess, Mother dumped the sweater into a foot tub of water to soak, hoping thus to salvage it on the morrow.

Between Easter and Whitsuntide, there were several spring rituals that we children of the neighborhood performed. I do not think of us as being botanists or zoologists, but we had a certain unintellectual knowledge of the fauna and flora about our countryside. Since we lived in the out-of-doors as much as farm time permitted, there came a natural awareness of the living things found in the orbit where we roamed. With this awareness came an appreciation of what we saw, and felt, and heard. So with the advent of spring, senses became more acute as life unfolded and moved about us. The woods and meadows provided many specimens for us to taste and feel and smell, to look at, and to wonder over.

One of our very favorite haunts was a dark, damp, cool woods about one half mile from our house. On the shady mossy hillsides were great patches of blue crowfoot violets, standing so thick and so close together that they touched petals in friendly communion. I know of no other spot where they grow in such profusion. This is one of the rather rare varieties of violets, and one of the most beautiful, with their pale violet-blue petals above, two dark purple ones below and a tiny yellow seedlike center. On a Saturday afternoon (a no-school day) after Bertha, Ruth, and Mary had finished their big Saturday jobs, and Frances and I our little ones, we set out on foot to keep our yearly tryst with our violets. We spent a bit of time just standing and drinking in the beauty before us, and breathing in the freshness and fragrance of the woods and flowers. Then, we plopped down on the soft mossy carpet, feet stretched out in front of us, just to rest and relax in an environment where we could simply be idle for a time, if we liked. Times for just being idle were not exactly abundant on our farm. After these moments of repose, we performed a rite that had been a tradition with us for as many years as I can remember. We knelt—of necessity—for the lowly violets and each picked a handful to carry home to enjoy them a while longer and to brighten a somewhat austere and plain farmhouse. With all the careful management and hard work, an eighty-acre farm simply would not sustain the buying of frills and luxuries. Perhaps, it was advantageous for us to have to create and innovate our own sources of beauty and happiness.

After Mother had enjoyed the beauty and fragrance of our nosegays for a minute, someone produced a dish in which we could arrange and place them on the dining room table for all to admire, even the men; though it's probable that our busy farmers were seldom aware of our attempts to bring to our home some aesthetic touches.

On a busy Saturday morning in the week that followed, when each of us was at his particular job assignment, the telephone rang two longs and one short, the Pence's ring.

"I'll answer it."

"No, I'll answer it."

"No, let me do it."

Mary, who was performing the weekly washing and

cleaning of oil lamps, quickly dried her hands on her apron and dashed to the telephone first.

Frances D., on the other end of the line, asked, "Can you all come down this afternoon? I was over on the bluff this morning and I saw some flowers comin' out, and the sweet anise looked juicy and tender."

"Wait a minute, Frances, and I'll ask Mother. Mother! Frances wants us to come down this afternoon to go over to the Bowman's bluff and see the flowers. Can we go?"

"If you work hard and get all your jobs done, I guess it will be all right."

Mary conveyed this good news to Frances, said goodbye, and hung up the receiver. She then hastened back to her task of cleaning the lamps, which included: cleaning and trimming the wicks; washing the glass chimneys, which were often smoked, and finally, filling them with oil.

Tired, but anticipating a happy relaxing afternoon, we set off up the dusty road to Frances' house to meet her, and from thence to the bluff on the slope of Bowman's hill, where the others were to join us. Many lovely plant specimens were growing on this woodsy bluff. There were little blue bells with fine wiry stems (we called them hairbells), the rare dogtooth violets, bloodroots, sweet anise, hazelnut trees, and many other common varieties of plants.

"Hi, hey, hello, 'haddo'!" Greetings were quick and casual. We found new sweet anise plants with their reddish veined stems and pleasant sweetish taste. We broke off some and chewed them, enjoying the honey-sweet flavor, not unlike candy or chewing gum, which were scarce commodities in our households. We observed the tadpoles and minnows coming to life in the "crick" that ran along the foot of the bluff. We looked; we wondered; we learned in nature's classroom.

It was not to be expected that so many youngsters on a steep bluff in one afternoon could get by without some mishap, and so it was with us. The daredevil of our crowd was the victim in this incident. That was our Elizabeth B., who was always brave or foolhardy enough, depending on how one looks at it, to be the experimenter in any challenging situation. Growing along this bluff were some hazelnut saplings, which brought us back to this spot in the fall to gather their nuts. Now, Elizabeth had the bright idea that if she could bend one of these slim trees down far enough to get a good hold on it somewhere near the top, it would make a good swing. She finally managed to do just this, but the results were not as she had anticipated. Instead of having a swing with the ground beneath her by which she could propel herself back and forth, the flexibility and strength of the sapling tossed her far out from the bank, suspending her in midair, feet dangling. She held fast with all her might and main, legs jerking up and down like a puppet on a string, and screaming bloody murder.

"Help me! Somebody please help me, don't just stand there like a bunch of ninnys!"

The image that came to me as I watched in horror, was that of a tremendous spider suspended in space by his single thread. On that steep bluff there was no possible way for us to reach her, so Bertha in her resourcefulness, yelled, "Drop and pray!"

Elizabeth looked down; below her was the "crick," five feet or more away (it must have appeared to her to be at least twenty-five) with its soft, thick, gooey mud and cold spring water. Her arms tired, and there being no other alternative, she dropped; if she obeyed the second command and prayed, it was not audible. She landed bottoms down in the chilly water and muddy depths below. Perchance the frogs had not awakened before from their winter's sleep, they certainly must have done so at that thunderous entrance into their sanctuary. The only wounds that Elizabeth seemed to have suffered were to her pride in the apparent nonsuccess of her bold stunt. If no prayer was uttered, her guardian angel must have been protecting her anyway, as it must have done many times thereafter in her life; else she would not be an alive grown woman today. As you must already know, she was wet from her top to her toes.

Margaret scolded, "Elizabeth, you'd better hurry home

and get off those wet dirty clothes before you get sick! I bet you'll get a good whippin'!" And thus ended our afternoon.

Then came May Day. Ours was not the old traditional English celebration of depositing little baskets of flowers on people's doorsteps and then disappearing, as practiced some places, even in the New World. We celebrated because there had long been a thought among us that it was safe for children to take off their shoes and go barefoot beginning May first. So out came our feet: to feel free, to wriggle toes, to run unhampered, to spread, to grow broad and flat and too big for our shoes come fall.

May Day was followed shortly thereafter by Whitsuntide. We have tried to find an answer for our going to the river on the Monday following Whitsunday. Research only told me that Whitsuntide is the season of Pentecost, comprising the week following Whitsunday, Whitsunday being the seventh Sunday or fiftieth day inclusive after Easter and so corresponding with Pentecost. So no answer to my question.

Sometime on the Monday following this Sunday, after our work was done, we children walked to the river, as also did many other residents of the community. There was quite a gathering. Some people say it was a day for fishing; but we did not fish. Some say it had a religious tradition somewhere in the past; but we were not a liturgical church and did not conform to the liturgical calendar in our beliefs and practices. Others said we went just from habit; in other words, we always had gone.

None of these answers seemed to quite fit our pattern; we just simply strolled along the river banks chatting with friends and looking at the spring flowers—the violets, the cowslips, and others with unknown names. So I have to conclude that we really had no known rationale for following this tradition—but then there was no rationale for many things we did as children on our farm.

CHAPTER 5

PRICKING NEEDLES

Summer came in on barefeet and school's end, not on the proverbial "lazy hazy days" of June. It brought with it freedom from confinement and studies. There was more time for relaxation and leisure—leisure for reading books, for activities with our friends, for swimming in the "cricks," playing games, exploring the fields, the meadows, and the woods; and hopefully, taking a trip as far as Harrisonburg ten miles away.

With the exhilaration that pervaded our emancipated bodies, minds, and spirits, we forgot for the moment that life on the farm inexorably moves on with its struggles and its toil, with its frailties and its uncertainties, with its times of heat and droughts and storms. But this moment was ours and it was a time for forgetting the difficult and rejoicing in the pleasant.

The next day following school closing, we were brought back to the realities of this life by Mother's voice. "Last evening as I was hoeing in the garden, I noticed that the peas looked like they were ready to eat. Bertha, you and Esther go out and pick a mess for dinner before the sun gets too hot. I think you can groovel under the potato hills and find a few new potatoes to cook with them. Also, pull up a few spring onions and radishes and cut some lettuce while you are there. They will taste mighty good for dinner."

We couldn't disagree with that; we had already been eating onions, radishes, and lettuce, and now, to add peas and new potatoes would delight every member of the family. However, I was less enthusiastic about the picking part, for I had other schemes for the morning already formulating in my head, if I could get Frances to cooperate. For the time being, these had to be put aside. When Pappy or Mother laid out plans and instructions for the tasks we must perform, we had somehow learned that arguing or grumbling was not very effective.

So donning sunbonnets, which we quite often did, to shield us from the hot summer sun, Bertha and I, with bucket and knife in hand, set off to the garden on our first assignment for the morning. My personal plans were put off for the time being, but not put out of mind.

The weather had been good to us this spring, sending us a generous amount of rain; so the peas on the vines were young and tender, the radishes—red and brash, the onions—juicy and sweet. Bertha was concerned that I learn the proper performance of chores. "Now, Esther, be sure the pods are filled well before you pick them."

"I know, I know!" I retorted, taking umbrage at the innuendo that I lacked the knowledge and skill to do this.

Up and down the two rows we went, one on each side, picking the fat ones and taking care not to shake off the blossoms of future ones. After having picked what Bertha considered would be sufficient for a mess of peas, which was at the least a half bucketful, I trudged behind her across the rough ground, my bare feet sinking deep into the soft tilled soil. In the onion patch we pulled a dozen or more new spring onions; next to them was the radish row where we picked the most fully developed ones. Finally, we cut the light-green tender lettuce leaves.

Bertha, reviewing our mental shopping list, asked, "Now let's see, do we have everything? Aw no, we forgot the potatoes. Esther, run to the house and get a pan to put them in." Wanting to oblige mostly because I still had in mind my project planned for the morning, I quickly complied.

After returning with the pan, we surveyed the potato patch to find the hills that seemed to be the most fully developed. Then we grooveled them out by snaking our hands under these hills to find the potatoes that were the largest, thereby leaving the rest undisturbed to continue their growth. At last, standing for a few minutes to straighten our tired backs which were stiff from stooping over for so long, we gathered together all our garden marketing for the day and proceeded to the house.

"Now," I thought, "I have finished my morning's work so I'll get Frances and go play for awhile." Not so!

Upon our return, Mother said, "Bertha, I know you and Esther are tired from all that stooping over in the heat, so we'll let you two sit on the back porch and cool off while you shell the peas. Mary is busy ironing; Ruth is working out the bread; Elizabeth and I have other things to do here in the kitchen."

"Boy, oh boy! Work! Work! Work! Nothing but old hard work!" I thought in disgust, but the peas were shelled and I helped.

Mother, turning to Frances and me, finally said, "Girls, it will be a while until dinner is ready since things have to cook, so you may go and play until then."

Still tired and irritable, I stalked off to our corner of the yard under the pear trees now full blown with leaves, thus providing a shady private workshop for us.

The day before, Mother had discarded some worn-out zinc can tops, and I had rescued them from the junk pile with a purpose already developing in my mind. Laying a board across some old unused bricks, we had a satisfactory work table for squatters. We had no interest in conforming to our farm kitchen schedule in which Saturday was the regular baking day—today was a fine day for mudpies. Dirt was a plentiful commodity; therefore we had no problem getting the ingredients for our pastry.

"Frances, you go to the cistern and pump this can full of water, and I'll dig up some dirt."

Dirt and water—what a simple recipe! Using sticks and our broken-handled spoon, we soon mixed it to what seemed the right consistency. The next step of pouring this mixture into our row of can tops having been accomplished, we were ready to test our creative art and skill. Perhaps we developed a little ingeniousness out of necessity, since we had few toys and materials to work with. In our search for possibilities, we noticed some wild daisies blooming along the wire fence that bordered the back of the yard, and our problem was solved.

"Frances, let's get some daisies to decorate our pies with; we can use the white petals and yellow centers."

"That's a good idea."

"We can use the petals and make coconut pies," I continued.

"And the yellow centers to make lemon pies; they are my favorite," suggested Frances.

Having collected our decorative material, we set to work with all the culinary art we could muster. We made lemon pies from the powdery yellow stamen, and we used the symmetry of an engineer in making designs with the daisy petals on our coconut pies. Placing the last petals, we surveyed our handiwork with some satisfaction.

"Don't they look pretty? I wish Mother and the girls could see them! Maybe they can later."

Frances said, drooling, "They look good enough to eat and that makes me think how hungry I am."

At that statement a diabolical thought entered my mind, and perhaps, still feeling a bit irritable at having my plans thwarted earlier, I said, "Try eating one of those lemon pies. It might taste good."

"I don't believe that it would be very good, Esther, would it?"

"I'll wave my fairy wand over it and change it by magic, like I read about in those stories in *Grimm's Fairy Tales*." Having proposed this, I proceeded to imitate the fairy godmother as I could best interpret.

"Now try it, Frances. If you eat one, I'll eat one," knowing full well my bluff would work and I wouldn't have to fulfill this promise.

Frances said hesitatingly, "I don't know about it." But curiosity and hunger were winning over her good judgment, so she picked up one of the bright yellow lemon pies and almost automatically took a sizable bite.

"Aa—aaa—aa! Tu—ey, tu—ey, tu—ey! Psh! Psh! Bah! Esther, why did you tell me to do that?"

"I was just playing with you."

69

At that precise moment, Mother's voice came to us from the house, "Girls, dinner is ready! Come in right away!"

Instantly we brushed off hands on our dresses and raced to the house, forgetting mudpies—looks, taste, and all.

"Frances, what in the world is that all over your mouth?" asked Mother.

Frances started to cry. "Esther m—ma—made me e—eat a m—mudpie!"

"I did not make you, Frances! You ate it yourself!"

"You said a—a—after yo—ou used m—magic on it, that it wo—wo—would taste g—good, but it didn't," still sobbing. "And yo—you said, if I ate on—on—one, you w—would too! You didn't do th—th—at either!"

Mother scolded, "Esther, aren't you ashamed of yourself treating your little sister like that? I ought to spank you! Now both of you wash up and come on to dinner. We are having those new peas and potatoes you helped gather this morning, Esther."

When Mother mentioned new peas and potatoes, a thought came to me, probably in self-justification. "Maybe the peas, potatoes, and onions would taste even better to Frances after sampling mudpies. What did everyone get so fussed up about?"

This summer, which began as a very usual one for us and our neighbors, took on a different aspect with an event that brought with it anxiety and apprehension. One Tuesday morning, which was ironing day on most farms in our neighborhood, we were all busily at work as customary. Bertha and Ruth were occupied with the tasks of washing the dishes, making up the beds, and performing the general cleaning of the morning. Elizabeth was doing the special cleaning in the parlor, where she received her beau when he came calling. Mother was in the kitchen already at preparations for dinner, and Mary and I had the Tuesday ironing job. Mary had set up the folding ironing board and I had spread out some cloths which served as a pad on the end of the dining table. She was preparing to iron the "fine" clothes which had been previously starched and "dampened down," not with a ready-mixed or spray-on type from a box or bottle, but homemade by cooking a batter of flour and water until thickened. Since I was younger and had not yet attained maximum efficiency, I was assigned the coarse clothes (everyday clothes)—men's overalls and shirts, bed clothes, towels, underdrawers. The four black irons had been placed on the stove earlier for heating (pre-electricity days for us). Mary and I got pads to hold their hot handles by and began. We would press until one iron had cooled down and was no longer efficient; then back to the stove for re-heating it went, and another one chosen, and the process of constantly alternating went on.

Mary, turning to me, said, "Esther, if we work real hard and finish our ironing by dinner, maybe Mother will let us go in swimmin' this afternoon with Frances D. and the Bowmans."

"I'll iron as fast as I can, but these old overalls sure are hard to iron! I wish they didn't have so many metal buttons and buckles!"

"You oughta' try these starched clothes; you have to press so hard to get the wrinkles out."

As we continued with our chatter to help lighten our job, Mother added her cheerful voice from the kitchen. Mother loved to sing, and her voice still haunts my memory as I try to recall the old hymns and ballads that were a part of her repertoire.

"I love to steal awhile away, From every cumb'ring care; . . ."*

At the moment all this activity was in progress, the first and only car in our neighborhood came chugging up the road.

Frances, who was in the kitchen puttering around with Mother, shouted, "A car is comin'! A car is comin'! Uncle Charlie is drivin' up the road!"

Out the door and across the porch she ran to climb on

---

*The Brethren Hymnal, House of the Church of the Brethren, Elgin, Illinois, 1882, 1901, 1952.

the lower rail of the paling fence, my eyes wistfully following her.

Climbing out of his car, Uncle Charlie asked, "Frances, where is your Mother?"

"In the kitchen," and with that she trotted around the house to the back porch with short, stocky, Dutchy Uncle Charlie following along.

"Mother, here's Uncle Charlie!" she called.

"Good morning, Brother Charlie. Let me dry my hands and then we'll go and sit in the front room. I'll be glad for a few minutes to cool off," Mother suggested.

Uncle Charlie, who was usually jovial and cheerful and loved to visit with Mother, seemed on this morning to be preoccupied and apprehensive, and he wasted little time in explaining his errand.

"Sister Mary, I have bad news. Annie Smith has the typhoid fever. I hated to render such a diagnosis, but I am quite sure about it. It has a very characteristic odor that one can smell when he enters the sick room. She is quite ill."

The Smiths lived down the road a few hundred yards from us on the farm that joined ours to the east.

"I am concerned about your family, for while we don't yet know the source of the infection, you are close enough for it to be carried by the flies. So I think the best thing to do is to give all of you the typhoid shots."

"You mean right now?"

"Yes, I think we'd better start right away. You will have to take three doses; we'll give one a week. So if the girls will round up the men, we'll start at once."

Mary and I, still ironing in the dining room, heard this disturbing unhappy news.

Mary exclaimed, "That's awful!"

"I'll say! I don't wanta' get stuck with any old needles!"

Shortly thereafter, Bertha and Ruth returned from the field with the men, and Uncle Charlie was ready to start inoculating.

"Where are Esther and Frances?" inquired Mother.

Jasper replied, "I kinda' think they slipped into the

washhouse a while ago. I'll see if I can get 'em." He did —grasping each one of us by an arm, dragging us in like pigs to be stuck for the slaughter.

The Pence's front room resembled a busy clinic that morning as we stood in a row with arms bared. In turns we submitted to the needle—some with resignation and some with reluctance. After other instructions on how to exercise precaution, Uncle Charlie chugged away in his little Ford runabout to continue his morning rounds.

After this crisis, there were no further thoughts or talk of going swimming for the day, with developing sore arms and emotional depression over concern for neighbors and fear for our own wellbeing. Also, Uncle Charlie had cautioned us against such activities for a day or two.

The hours passed more quietly than usual; our enthusiasm and energy were more subdued; our communication with each other was less vocal; and our activities less vigorous. The men returned to the fields; Ruth and Bertha to bed making and house cleaning; Elizabeth to shining the parlor. Mary and I finished the ironing. Mother completed dinner, but with no cheerful accompaniment of song.

As we sat on the front porch at the end of our work day, Mother suggested that we sing, perhaps to buoy everyone's spirits, or perhaps because she was aware that life moves on in spite of anxieties and problems. Singing signaled her efforts to return to normalcy.

"Let's start off with 'Twilight is Stealing.' We'll sing one verse."

> Twilight is stealing over the sea,
> Shadows are falling dark on the lea; . . .*

"Let's sing 'The Jealous Lover,'* the whole thing. I like that."

"Let's sing 'Mrs. Lofty.'* I wanta' sing all that, too. It's not very long."

---

*Glossary

73

Pappy asked, "Why don't you sing a hymn or two now? How about 'On Jordon's Stormy Banks'?"*

We fulfilled this request and then followed with "How Tedious and Tasteless the Hours,"** one of Mother's favorites.

At the end of this hymn, Mother suggested, "I guess it's about bedtime. Girls, have you washed your feet?"

Since we were barefooters, we, out of necessity, practiced feetwashing before bedtime. Our procedure was to get the tin foot tub, pump in a few inches of cold water from the cistern, and douse our feet and legs up to our knees or thereabouts. This was not a scrubbing in any sense, but rather a sort of rinsing and flushing that perhaps took away some of the more obvious dirt and discoloration.

"I washed mine earlier," I answered.

Frances said, "So did I."

"You did not, Frances."

"I did too."

"Frances, let me look at your feet," ordered Mother.

Frances, sheepishly, said, "I guess I forgot."

"Go wash your feet, Frances."

The healthy energy of youngsters cannot be locked in at any length by emotional depression, and so it was with us. In the days that followed, we worked and played as vigorously as ever when we were not limited by sore arms, or the slight fevers and headaches which accompanied our injections.

One evening at the supper table Pappy announced, "Jasper and I were looking over the wheat fields today, and we decided the wheat is ready to cut. I think we'll begin now while the weather is favorable and the ground is dry."

So it was, that the next morning as soon as the dew had evaporated, Pappy checked over the binder (reaper) to see that everything was in good order, oiling it in all moving parts, and threading it with twine. In the mean-

---

*The Brethren Hymnal, 1882, 1901.

time, Jasper, by use of the cradle, cut the wheat in the corners where the binder was not maneuverable—no grain must be lost.

Then the three horses were hitched to the binder and all was ready. Frances and I were ready also—that is, we were ready to follow the binder over the field a round or two, for this method of cutting wheat was a very fascinating process. The great reel on the binder forced the wheat into the knife for cutting, and further caused it to fall in an orderly manner for tying in bundles, called sheaves. These were accumulated on a carrier then dumped by the operator at intervals in large heaps thus favoring the shockers. After the first two rounds, Jasper, Wilbur, and Jake began gathering the sheaves and standing them in shocks which usually contained ten or twelve of these bundles. The shock was capped by two sheaves, fanned out and placed with the first in one direction and the other in the opposite protecting the grain from rainwater.

At a safe distance, Frances and I trudged along behind the binder, fascinated by its motions and its click, click, clicking sound. No matter that freshly cut wheat stubbles scratched our legs and the clods were rough beneath our feet. No matter that Wilbur and Jake tried to torment us by shouting, "Why don't ya' get to work and help us shock wheat? You all don't ever do anything but just 'piddle' around."

Every day Pappy scanned the sky for weather signs, and observed the wind direction by the fan on the windwheel. In the evening, after two days of wheat cutting, he remarked, "The sun is setting red and the wind is from the west, so I believe good weather is going to prevail 'til we finish harvesting the wheat tomorrow."

As a weather prophet, our Pappy was not bad; and so it was that the next day the harvesting job was finished.

In the afternoon we children decided it was time for us to get in a swim before we had to take our next and final typhoid shot. Thus after telephoning and planning, the group gathered and hiked to the "crick" for something we called a swim, using that word in a very un-

75

restricted sense. After wading for a short time in the water up to our knees, which was not quite satisfying, we decided to go to our favorite spot, "The Big Rock."

That meant a longer walk down through the meadows, but we were accustomed to that, so away we went picking our way through the patches of nettle and thistle. On arrival we immediately jumped, and to our delight, we were in water up to our crotches instead of our knees! Our dresses, which were our swim suits, ballooned out around us. We jumped up and down and in and out; we stood on our heads and somersaulted in our unpolluted water. We tried swimming, diving, and floating in the two-foot depth.

"Look how I can swim!" we shouted, fanning feet and arms up and down with obvious splashing, but with little perceptible progress. The skill developed was not commensurate with the effort, but the joy we felt made it all worthwhile.

"Watch me dive!" we cried, pointing hands and head in the right direction, but still managing to land with feet down and head up. So we laughed and chatted and played.

Finally, concluding we ought to go "before it gets too late" (Mother's words), we reluctantly climbed out. As we usually did before leaving, we pulled the leeches from our legs, some having already penetrated the skin, bringing the blood. We stepped briskly along, the sun and the wind drying our clothes as we went.

When we neared our point of separation, Ruth suggested to our friends, "You all come over tomorrow afternoon or sometime soon; the early harvest apples are gettin' ripe. We have been fryin' the ones that drop and they are gettin' real good."

Our Pappy was a good orchardist, and the Pence orchard was the best in the whole community, maybe the whole county; perhaps he had the biggest incentive in his biggest family. That orchard was truly a marvel; beginning with the early harvest we had apples continuously until the season was over. After the early harvests were gone, the strawberry reds and longstems came, then the maidens blush, smokehouse, and northern spy. These were followed by the late fall apples picked for winter—winesaps, johnsons, and genettes. The latter were buried in the soil for winter keeping. The winesaps and johnsons were stored in the barn and cellar and provided apples for us all through months when other fresh fruits were scarce.

Our friends responded with,

"We'll try to come."

"I think Mother will let us."

"I'm hungry for those apples."

"Goodbye and come over."

That evening, our neighbor Mrs. Smith died, and another case of typhoid broke out in the family—daughter Ollie. Although we dreaded that hypodermic needle, actually we were relieved to be taking the last one the next day, for it would give us some sense of security against this frightening disease that was proving so disastrous to our neighbors. These recent events were presaging an uneasy disquieting summer for us.

CHAPTER 6

FLY BUSHES

"Children, get up right away! Have you forgotten it's Sunday and we'll have to step around to get to church on time? Quickly, girls! Boys! Get up and come on down to get your work done!" From above her head Mother could hear "Thump! Thump! Thump, thump!" as we popped out of bed one by one and two by two and she knew her command was being obeyed.

The farm was soon alive with motion and the clamor of activity. Going to church on Sunday mornings was looked to with anticipation. By today's measurements that may seem "square" and old-fashioned, but traveling even a few miles from the homestead to be with others and to participate in a larger gathering was a pleasant interlude. Finally, we were all dressed in our Sunday best, our faces, hands, feet, bodies, and hair clean and shining from our weekly Saturday night baths of the evening before.

Saturday evening bath scheduling required some expertise. In a house without bathing facilities and running water, the tin washtub took on importance after supper when a dozen human bodies needed their weekly cleansing. The teakettle and buckets full of water were placed on the stove to heat for that purpose. With knees propped up to our chins in order to fit into the tub, we scrubbed as best we could in our three- to four-inch ration of water. As the consequence of a community's Saturday night baths and change of clothes, the atmosphere of our church on Sunday mornings must have been more pleasant than our schoolrooms on Fridays.

Now horses were hitched to the surrey and to the buggy and tied just outside the gate, ready for us to climb aboard and ride the three miles to our church. That surrey was our pride and joy; it was the most pretentious piece of equipment the Pences owned, albeit, a very necessary one. It was commodious with two red, plush, cushioned seats, fringe on the top, and lanterns on either side in front. Pulled by a team of horses, it could carry a goodly number of the family. Frances had a place of honor with Mother and Pappy in front, sometimes squeezing in between and sometimes leaning against Mother's plump knees. The four older girls graced the back in their pretty homemade dresses; while I stood in front of them holding on to the front seat. As I stood, my eyes were directly in line with my Pappy's white celluloid collar fitted inside his buttoned-up coat. I was fascinated with the patterns formed by the little lines and furrows in his neck above it as they shifted in rhythm with the movement of the surrey. I was tempted to take my finger and trace these little channels as they followed his neck

78

around and disappeared under his white bearded chin. My eight-year-old judgment told me that it would not be exactly advisable, so I refrained by clutching the back of his seat the more tightly.

The three boys drove ahead in the buggy, wanting to speed a little at ten or twelve miles per hour. Thus in "style" we drove into the churchyard, tied our horses to the long hitching rail, and moved into the long plain church.

Here we joined our fellow worshippers in hymn singing without instrumental accompaniment, scripture reading, prayer, and listening to a sermon. To the right of the pulpit were the benches where the deacons, ministers, and elders sat (including my Pappy) in their plain buttoned-up coats and no ties; many with full beards. In the main part and to the right was the section reserved for the men and boy children. To the left was the section for ladies only. Many of them, including my Mother, wore dark long dresses and capes, with their little white prayer veils or caps atop their neatly brushed hair and serene faces. Here, the smaller girls sat with their mothers until they reached the age of responsibility, at which time they were allowed to join friends in the raised seat section on either side of the main floor. Frances and I had not yet reached this state of maturity, thus we sat with our Mother. We were a most segregated church—by sex only.

On this particular morning, it was our Pappy's time to preach; and his clear, strong, resonant voice penetrated every corner and crevice of the church. In spite of this, or perhaps because it was our Pappy's voice, Frances went sound asleep with her head on Mother's lap; and I, leaning against her arm, had almost joined my sis in slumberland before the final hymn and closing prayer. None of the preachers of our church, including our Pappy, were paid pastors, but were called to the ministry by the congregation—and presumably by the Lord, also.

On the way home, Elizabeth remarked, "Pappy, I thought that was a good sermon you preached this morning."

Bertha added, "So did I, but I didn't understand what you meant when you talked about 'being saved by faith.' Is that all we hafta' do to be saved; just have faith?"

"When we get home, we'll read the scripture on it, and I'll explain it to you," promised Pappy.

Mary interjected, "I was glad you didn't preach an hour like Mr. Long does."

"Frances didn't know what you said, Pappy, 'cause she went to sleep," I added.

Mother reminded me, "I don't think you heard much either, Esther, for you were about asleep, too."

I was a bit squelched at that and could make no further comment.

Our friends accepted our apple-eating invitation and came the next week. We swarmed over our early harvest trees as bees did for the nectar at blossom time, choosing the ripest and biggest apples we could spot. After picking the quantity we considered might satisfy our afternoon appetites, the older girls: Bertha, Ruth, Mary, and Frances D., sat on the ground with their laps full of apples. The little ones, Ruth and Virginia, cuddled close to them to be near the apple supply. Margaret, Elizabeth, Frances, and I sat on a broad, low, flat limb that was just made for sitting, our feet dangling and swinging beneath us. This tree was a very special tree, and it, too, holds a favored place in our memories as the spot for many interesting conversations and the expressions of unrecorded hopes and dreams.

We sat and chatted and munched, filling our tummies fuller and fuller. It was a warm, lazy, relaxing afternoon and we took advantage of our shade and cool grass. In the field by the orchard, Jasper was mowing hay and we could hear his "Gees! Haws!" and "Git ups, Chester and Morg!" in the distance, as faint sweet odors of the new mown hay came to us through the fruit-laden trees.

Ruth asked, "Did you all know that Ollie Smith died this morning? She is going to be buried Thursday."

Ollie was the Smith's married daughter who lived at

her parents' home which was not uncommon in those days.

"Isn't that awful? I'm scared!" said Mary, expressing her fears.

Others exclaimed, "We are too!"

"Do you reckon they had a token of her death?" asked Margaret.

"No, of course not. There's no such thing as a token of someone's death!" Bertha replied emphatically.

Frances D. retorted just as emphatically, "There is so such a thing! Whenever anyone in my Grandma's family died, our big old Grandfather's clock, which hadn't been runnin' for years and years, would strike before he died. It struck before my Grandpa and my mother died."

"Maybe a mouse or somethin' was in the clock. Our parents said things like that don't happen," Ruth tried to explain.

Margaret countered, "They do, too! My mother told us about a piano playin' all by itself. No one was in the room. It was just before someone died."

"Did your Mother hear it?" I asked.

"No, Esther."

"Then how do you know it happened?"

Frances D. offered more proof. "And Grandma told me about a little white bird that flew into a child's room before the child died."

"I think people just imagine those things. My Pappy says when the time comes for people to die, they die, but that God doesn't scare them halfway there first," Mary said with some finality.

At that point, the argument was stopped before it got any more heated and a falling out occurred among life-long friends. However, our spats and arguments were certainly not unusual, and they seldom lasted until we played together again. Anyhow, at that moment, Jasper who became aware that we were in the orchard eating apples stopped his mower, came to the fence, and called to us, "Girls, bring me a coupla' apples to eat; and I want to tell you something. A few minutes ago while I was mowin', a meadow lark flew straight up in front of me and I knew I was close to her nest; so I mowed around it leavin' a patch of grass to protect her home."

In those days any good farmer had a respect for nature and all its creatures; life was his ecology teacher.

Ruth suggested, "We haven't eaten all our apples, Esther, why don't you and Frances get a 'poke' and take some to Pappy and Wilbur and Jake who are hoein' corn in the field behind the barn?"

Since the mother-assigned hour had come for our friends to depart, we were willing to comply.

By now we were truly enjoying our orchard and garden. It was the time of strawberry red and long stem apples and our own private supermarket was supplying us with daily menus of new corn, tomatoes, beans, and cabbage. We pulled corn, shucked it, and threw it immediately into the pan. We cooked our beans for a long time in a black iron pot with a sugar-cured ham hock and new potatoes added later. We knew the full measure of the simple goodness of fresh vegetables. But the blessings of farm life seldom come easy, thus most of our days were filled with difficult time-consuming jobs. The garden had to be weeded and hoed. We had to conserve the moisture in the ground as best we knew how; there were no recent rains and a summer drought seemed to be setting in. Then, of necessity, all the vegetables and fruits that were not consumed on the daily table had to be preserved for the long winter months ahead. We dried the extra corn by cutting it off the cob, spreading it on a cloth on screen wire and placing it in the sun to dry. It had to be stirred occasionally and never allowed to get wet by the rain. The leftover tomatoes were cooked in an open kettle and put in cans while they were hot. No cold pack or deep freeze methods were known to us in those days.

Apples covered the ground under our trees in profusion; neighbors were invited in to help themselves. They came, filling buckets and sacks as full as they could carry. Pappy and Mother always took special care to see that the Smiths had a continuous supply since they were under strict quarantine. This made it difficult to sustain our normal neighborly relations of sharing and visiting with each other.

Then apple "schnitzing" (cutting into pieces) time was upon us. Bushels were peeled, schnitzed, and spread on a metal roof to dry. Gathering them off a hot tin roof that had been exposed to the sun all day, if rain threatened, was a painful chore even to our toughened feet! After these schnitz were dried, they were sacked and stored in a dry place for winter stewing and for use as schnitz 'n dumplings.

Our parents tried to provide a few compensations, however small, for the hard work they required of their children. Thus whenever the apple crop was bountiful, time was available, and the older girls were ambitious enough, Mother permitted them to schnitz some and sell them to obtain a little spending money of their very own. So after their project was completed, they would drive off in a buggy to Yager's Store with their precious cargo to trade for extra school supplies such as pencils and tablets, maybe a bit of lace or ribbon for trimming a dress, or some other small object they desired. Occasionally, they would offer Frances and me a bribe of a couple of pennies to assist them in the schnitzing. More often though, we might be found on a money-making campaign of our own. We scavenged over the fields and buildings for bits of scrap iron and bones to be sold for a few pennies to the Junk and Hide Company of Harrisonburg.

There are numerous ways of earning or acquiring a bit of money for oneself, and Frances discovered one of them.

One morning Mother asked, "Esther, would you and Frances like to go to the store with me in a little bit? I have to get some sugar and spices for canning, coal oil for the lamps, and a few other items. You can keep me company."

"Yes, yes, yes!" we said, bouncing up and down, forward and backward, sideways and into everything and everybody.

"Go wash your faces and hands then, and let Bertha

83

comb your 'stroobly' (tousled) heads." This time we willingly submitted to this ordeal without squawking.

Soon we were off in the buggy accompanied by two non-laying hens with feet tied, lying in the storage compartment behind, and a basket of eggs at our feet. This produce was to be traded for items Mother intended to buy. We moved along at an easy gait, chatting about small things and observing the scenery about us.

Just before arriving at the store, Mother asked, "Esther, did I ever tell you about the time you got lost and frightened us so terribly? Driving to the store brought it to mind."

"No, but tell us right now; I want to hear about it."

"I won't have time now, for we are almost at the store. Remind me when we start home and I will."

On our arrival, Mother went with Mr. Yager into the receiving and storage room where he weighed the chickens, counted the eggs, and calculated their worth in trade. While this transaction was being made, Frances and I drifted into the main part of the store. Frances quickly moved to the glass candy case, laid two pennies on the counter, and asked for two cents worth of candy. Mr. Pirkey, the clerk, put several pieces of hard candy in a small paper poke and handed it to her; then she slipped to a secluded corner of the store. Frances, who was not accustomed to using much finesse in her actions, was not aware that my covetous eyes were following her. I immediately stalked her into her corner, where she had already poked a piece of candy into her mouth and was sucking it with noisy vigor and pleasure.

"Frances, where did you get those pennies?"

Sheepishly, she answered, "I didn't put them in the collection last Sunday at Sunday School."

"Mother will sure get you for that. I won't tell her though, if you'll give me some of the candy."

Caught in a trap, Frances reluctantly gave me a couple pieces of her supply now diminishing faster than she liked. My attempts at juvenile blackmail were successful. While Mother purchased her necessities, Frances and I

84

wandered around the store peeking into this and that, admiring and wishing.

As we started home, Mother learned anew that children seldom forget promises when we reminded her almost immediately that we were ready to hear the story about my getting lost.

Mother's Story

One summer day about like today when you were not quite three years old, Esther, I was getting ready to go to the store, just as I did this morning. You wanted to go along but it didn't suit to take you, so I said 'No.' I left you and Frances at home in the care of your older sisters. Frances was still a little toddler and she was no problem. But, Esther, you were very cross, and so you pouted and cried after I left. Sometime later, the older girls missed you and began calling and looking, but couldn't find you. Finally they got scared and went to the fields to check with the men. You were not there, so the men left their work right away to join in the hunt. Thinking that you might have gone with me after all, Jasper bridled a horse and took off up the road at a fast gallop, to check. When I saw him coming I knew something was wrong and he lost no time in asking, 'Mother, is Esther with you?' After he told me that you couldn't be found anywhere, I slapped my horse with the lines and drove home faster than I ever drove in my life.

By the time I got home, they had checked with the neighbors, who were now joining in the search. They looked in the buildings and the fields; they went to the 'crick' and the woods; they looked in all the possible little hideaways on the farm. Pappy, who had a very strong voice, climbed to the top of the high windwheel and called and called, 'Esther! Esther! Esther!' No answer. By this time, everyone was really scared and upset, for we simply didn't know which way to turn next. So we began going back and lookin' in all the places where we had been before. Pappy's trip took him again through the chicken yard where the chicken coops were, you know, where the mother hens raise their broods of little ones. One coop had been turned upside down sometime or other and was resting on its roof. Your Pappy just happened to glance over into this upside down coop—and guess what? There you were, Esther, scrunched down in one corner, sound asleep. Pappy shouted, " 'Here she is! I found her!' "

After all the worries of the morning were gone, I think everybody cried a little for joy that you were safe and sound.

I sighed with relief, too, as Mother ended the story, "I sure am glad Pappy found me!"

So far as we know, that was Frances' last attempt to cheat the Lord by withholding her pennies; for on the next Sabbath afternoon in Sunday School Class I watched as she dropped her two cents into the collection cup. We had walked the two miles to our little white church called Sunnyside, as we had done for many years whenever the weather permitted. This was known as a preaching point of Mill Creek, our Mother Church; however, we did not drive to the big church with regularity, so much of our religious training was made possible at this nearer church. We met Frances D. at our crossroads, and a half mile farther on, we picked up the Bowmans at the end of their lane.

In our little class in one corner of this church, we put our pennies in the collection, said our Bible verses for which we received little gay colored tickets, and listened to the Bible story of the day. Following this, we all moved into the main section for worship and preaching.

While this service was in progress, a little event occurred that is still vivid in my memory. During the singing of the hymns when we were about halfway through "Beulah Land," I happened to glance down at my dress. "O my gracious! This is awful!" In that instant I realized that my dress was on wrong side out. The big thick seams that were made in most clothes in those days stood out like the ridges on a washboard. In my mortification and desperation I "rootshed" around trying to hide them, which was all but impossible. So my only hope was that no one would notice until I got home and could change. When we finally made it through "Beulah Land," we knelt to pray, turning and facing our benches as we did so. I am certain my prayer was concerned more about help for concealing my dreadful mistake than it was for the "poor benighted heathen" in India or Africa. I think the Lord must have heard the prayers of one little embarrassed girl that day, for much to my surprise and relief, no one ever noticed. But I clearly remember that little blue and white checked dress with the thick double seams and a little black velvet bow at the neck.

On the way home we talked about a very serious and solemn subject, expressing the thoughts of our parents in our conversation as youngsters are wont to do. World War I was still being fought and the fact that Charlie, our brother, had been drafted was often on our minds and in our conversations.

Bertha, in a serious mood, said, "We haven't heard from Charlie for a while and it worries Mother and Pappy, so I wish this war would soon be over. They've had enough worries this summer with the typhoid fever at the Smiths' and the drought and everything. Did you know that Ruth Nair has the fever now?"

Frances D., with emphasis, cried, "I hate war! Why do people have to fight and kill each other anyway?"

"Our Pappy says Our Church believes that war is wrong, and we believe that, too. He says it never makes things better and that we ought to settle our differences in a peaceful way and get along with other people," continued Ruth.

Wilbur, looking at it from a boy's viewpoint, said, "I sure hope it gets over soon, for I'd sure hate to have to go and get shot or shoot somebody else."

Margaret, from a girl's viewpoint, said, "I'm sure glad girls don't have to go to war."

"I wonder if it will be over soon. I hope so. Pappy

said he thinks President Wilson hopes so, too," I added.

Having finally exhausted our supply of comments on the subject, we began singing the hymns of the afternoon, including "Beulah Land," which served as an unwelcome reminder of my earlier embarrassing experience.

Wilbur, addressing Frances D. and the Bowmans, said, "Jake and I just finished making a new stringball this week. Can't you all go along and play a game of Roun' Town?"

Roun' Town must have surely been the forerunner of baseball; except that we were more free to make up our own rules, which we quite often did; our ball was made of string, but no leather cover; our bat was simply a narrow plank with a handle at one end carved by a few chops of the ax for better gripping.

Frances D. replied, "I guess we can, but not for very long."

With her statement, we walked down the road a bit more rapidly.

When we arrived at our front gate, we scarcely noticed the buggy and horse hitched there, nor that Elizabeth, dressed in her finest, was being helped in by her beau.

We quickly rounded up all playing candidates, including Pappy, which almost made two teams. Choosing up sides, we proceeded to play with all the shouting, coaching, arguing, and individual umpiring of modern day baseball.

"Can't you throw it over the plate?"

"Hit it, Jake!"

"Run, Mary!"

"Catch it, Elizabeth!"

"Throw the ball to me, quick!"

"You're out!"

"I'm not!"

"You are!"

"I'm not!"

On and on and on.

The days continued to pass without rain. The hay was cured and hauled into the mow for storage; the wheat had thoroughly dried and had been conveyed to the barn wagonload after wagonload on specially-made framework called "ladders." Soon it would be threshed and the grain taken to the mill for marketing, less the portion that would be ground for our year's supply of flour. Pappy scanned the sky every day and checked the wind directions for signs of rain. Our gardens and pasture lands were beginning to suffer from lack of water.

On Tuesday, Pappy announced to the family that the farmers in the neighborhood had planned a schedule for threshing wheat since the man who owned and operated the threshing equipment would be in our area this week. He continued, "They should be at our place on Thursday morning. Mother, we'll have to fix dinner for them."

It took a number of "hands" to thresh a mow full of wheat, so instead of hiring help, the farmers would assist each other by following the work from one farm to the next and the next. The distaff side of the household had to be about its pots and pans and crockery from the time of Pappy's announcement until the food would be blessed and eaten.

Mother began immediately to make plans. "Girls, one of the jobs we need to do before Thursday is to make new fly bushes. It should have been done earlier, as the old ones are about worn out, but we just didn't seem to get to it. Esther, you can help the older girls with this; each of you can make one."

If one of those fly bushes were to find its way into a present-day classroom, it would pass for a piece of creative modern art work. For us, it had a very practical use. Each assignee took one of the old bushes from the corner of the dining room safe. First, we stripped off all the old paper from the round sticks cut from tree branches. Next, we held a couple thicknesses of fresh newspaper at their centerfold around the sticks and sewed them round and round in spiral fashion with a heavy needle and cord. Then this paper was cut in strips approximately one and one-half inches wide. Following that, these strips were folded in accordion-like pleats all the way to the stick—a frilly mass of paper, not unlike crinkly streamers of crepe paper, but much noisier. We swished them a few times to loosen and separate the strips, and they were ready for use.

We had first-hand knowledge of what it means to "eat like harvest hands." Preparing the meal was almost a full day's job, thus even the least of us was drafted for work. We cleaned chickens, cut them up and salted them down in crocks, which were then taken to the cellar to keep for the next day's frying. Beans, tomatoes, and potatoes were gathered from the garden. Corn would be plucked on the morrow to insure absolute freshness and taste. Frances and I were kept busy bringing in water from the cistern and emptying peelings and leftovers into the slop buckets that sat on a shelf under the grapevine.

We were glad to get away from the house and the heat as Mother gave us a new assignment. "You two girls take a coupla' buckets and bring in some apples from the orchard. We want to stew a dishful and make some pies."

So away we went to the cool and shade of the orchard where apples covered the ground in abundance. First, we each chose a fat, ripe, juicy one to eat, rubbed them off on our dresses and munched as we worked. We were in no hurry to return to the house, so we took our good time in filling the buckets, until we heard Mother's voice calling, "Girls, hurry with those apples!"

By the time we had returned with our buckets filled, I decided I had done enough work for a while, especially since I wanted to finish reading *Little Prudy* and *Little Prudy's Sister Sue*. So I set my bucket of apples on the porch and quietly and quickly slipped around the house, retrieved my book from the front steps where I had left it, situated myself comfortably on the porch swing, found my place, and began to read.

Shortly thereafter, I heard from the house, "Where's Esther? I need her to help me peel apples. Esther, where are you? We need you."

Then I did what children have always done since the beginning; I pretended not to hear and continued with my reading.

This time the voice was louder and more insistent, "Esther, I want you to come here right away; where are you hiding?"

Frances informed Mother, "I think she's on the front porch readin' a book. She sneaked around the house after we came in from the orchard."

Now I knew I'd better answer, "All right, I'm comin'."

"Now don't go away like that again, Esther. We still have things to do. You help Ruth and Mary peel apples; Frances, you can break the beans as Bertha strings them. Elizabeth and I need to get dinner on the table now, but maybe later on this afternoon we can have a few minutes for resting."

While we were busy in the house, the men were making other preparations for the morrow. They put the barn in good order and cut a generous supply of wood for firing the steam engine that drove the threshing machine.

Thus our day passed as hands and feet were kept busy much of the time. My mind was busy, too, and the thoughts that were there were those of a little girl who was just beginning to peep through a very small opening into the future and wondering if it might not be a bit more glamorous than the present with its almost daily quota of hard work. I wondered, "Are all Dutch People farmers and do they always have to work so hard? I hope I don't have to spend all my life scrubbin', and ironin', and sweepin', and doin' all those hard jobs. I want to do something else when I grow up. Maybe a movie star," though my ideas of such people were almost beyond the pale of my knowledge. I had never seen one of the silent films that were the ultimate in entertainment in those days. Not too many years later, I made my first entrance into a movie house and viewed, "A Man Without a Country"; not exactly a child's film.

My thoughts continued. "Maybe I could be a school teacher like my sister Elizabeth; but first I want to go to college most of all." Books were beginning to hold a terrible fascination for me and I wanted access to many more.

The threshing machine pulled into our place before dark in order to get an early start the next morning, so that meant off to bed for everyone before it was late.

When the sun peeped over the Blue Ridge the next morning, the farm was astir: breakfast was soon over; cows were milked and driven to the back pasture; dishes were washed; and the floors swept. The neighboring farmers arrived and the threshing began. In the house, dinner preparations began also: we brought corn from the garden, shucked it, and cut it off the cob to make a huge dishful; we started the beans cooking. The chickens were put in the black iron skillet for frying; potatoes were peeled; apples were stewed; tomatoes were placed in cold water to chill. We prepared a big container of lemonade and a pot of coffee was set on the stove to perk. Then we got our new-made fly bushes out of the corner by the safe, and Ruth and I began chasing the flies out of the dining room while Frances held open the screen door for us. We started on the side of the room opposite the door and moved toward it, shaking and rattling our bushes vigorously as we went. We repeated this operation several times, concluding finally that we had chased out most of the flies. Then moving to the kitchen, we repeated the process there.

At that moment, Jake appeared at the kitchen door, "Pappy said to tell you that they would finish the threshing before they would stop to eat. He said it would take about a half'n hour yet." This was quite satisfactory to the cooks, since it gave us time for setting the table and getting the food on.

Washpans, towels, soap, and a comb were carried out by the cistern for cleanup by the "hands." At approximately the set time, the shrill steam whistle on the engine sounded, announcing the completion of the Pence threshing job, and notifying the next neighbor that the workers would be on the way shortly.

The men hurried to the yard. They brushed their clothes, combed the chaff from their hair, and washed in the cold water from the cistern; then they were truly ready to eat. Pappy, tired and hungry, stopped by the kitchen to report with happiness that we had a good yield of wheat—four hundred forty-five bushels.

The men filed into the dining room and sat down at the table with no seating arrangements, no quibblings over where they would sit. Pappy having said his usual blessing, little sound was heard as they quickly began eating the food on the well-filled table; only an occasional, "Please pass the bread," "I'd like some more corn," "How about some chicken." These succinct remarks were mingled with the rather constant swish of our fly bushes trying to keep the few flies that had escaped us earlier away from the food. After the pie had been served and eaten, the men left almost as quickly and as silently as they came, in order to move on to the next farm and the next threshing job.

After the whirligig morning and meal, we took some time in the part of the day remaining for rest and relaxation; Bertha, Ruth, and Mary to reading or to cutting scraps for quilt squares; Frances to just puttering around; and I to engrossing myself with Little Prudy on the front porch.

On a farm, nature determines that there is a certain order in the performance of tasks. Thus it was on the day following threshing, we performed an assignment that was a part of this cycle—filling our bed ticks with freshly threshed straw.

Mother, after the family was up, said, "Girls, today I think we'd better empty our bed ticks, wash them while we have a good day for drying, and fill them with the new straw."

So the fire was built under the iron kettle in the wash-house and we filled it with water, in which we would boil the ticks with some scraps of soap. In the meantime, we carried them to the barnyard, opened one end, and thoroughly shook out the contents—straw that had been broken and almost beaten into chaff by the bodies that had "rootshed" around and slept on it for a year.

Then back to the washhouse, where we scrubbed each one on the washboard and dropped it into the kettle of hot water to boil. After fishing them out of the hot water with a long wooden stick, they were rinsed and hung out on the clothesline in the air and sun to dry.

By afternoon, they were ready to be filled with the freshly-threshed straw, so back to the barnyard we took them to the newly-formed strawrick. Gathering handfuls of the best straw, we stuffed and shoved, stuffed and shoved, until the ticks were enormous puffed-up blimps.

Mother was waiting at the house with coarse thread and needle to whip them shut. Finally, we carried them upstairs and placed them on our slat and rope beds (no springs) to be ready for retirement time. Frances and I surveyed the finished project with anticipation of the fun we would experience sleeping on this high mound for a night or two.

When bedtime came, no one had to tell us the second time, "Go to bed, girls." Up the stairs we raced, pulling off our dresses as we went; in the summertime we slept only in our brown cotton-cloth drawers. We climbed up one side of the high rounded tick to slide down the opposite, the original chute-the-chute. Round and round we went, up one side and down the other.

Frances shouted, "This is fun!"

"It sure is!" But now ready for a new experiment, I said, "I bet I can jump from our bed over on to Bertha's and Ruth's." With that statement I sprang like a kangaroo, sailed across and landed on target making a considerable depression in their straw tick as I did so.

"Let me try it, too! Get outa' the way, Esther!" and over she came. But as she landed, down came one of the slats under the tick with a resounding clatter on the floor.

Mother from downstairs, demanded, "What are you all doin' up there? You girls go to bed right away."

Mary said disgustedly, "I bet they're messin' up our beds."

By the time we had climbed to the top of our mound

and burrowed in a little, hoping not to roll off before morning, the older ones lumbered upstairs to bed.

Ruth said crossly, "You bad girls! Look what you did to our beds! You need a good spankin'!"

In disgust, they lifted the tick, picked up the fallen slats and arranged all of them evenly on the bed, then replaced the tick. By the time they had undressed and settled down, Frances and I were asleep on our mountain top with the smell of fresh straw in our nostrils, but unaware of its prickly roughness beneath us.

When one is a child, time seems to move slowly, but to my Mother and Pappy this summer must also have passed slowly. The July and August drought had been a rather extended and severe one. The typhoid fever that resulted in the loss of neighbors and its attendant danger to our family must have often brought unexpressed apprehension to them. But now summer was almost gone, and September was on the launching pad with happier days aboard.

One morning Uncle Charlie's runabout stopped at the front, and as he appeared at the door, it was apparent that he was in a happier mood than at an earlier time.

"Sister Mary, children, I have good news for you. It looks like we have Ruth Nair and Ike on the road to recovery at last. Also, we have located the source of infection; their well was found to contain the typhoid bacteria. Now that cooler weather will soon be on the way, maybe you can begin to relax a bit, but continue to exercise a little care. Get your rest and stay as healthy as you can."

He sat and cheerfully talked a while, and we girls all hung around to listen as we usually did when friends or relatives would drop by for a few minutes. This was one of the pleasant diversions of farm life.

Pappy was hopeful when evening came as he made this observation, "The wind has been blowing from the southeast all day and now the sun is setting behind a bank of gray clouds—we might just have rain tomorrow. That sure would be a blessing."

"One, two, three! Here I go!" shouted Elizabeth B., as she propelled herself out of the upper back barn door into the newly-made strawrick.

"And one, two, three! Here I go!" shouted Wilbur, whose turn was next, followed by Jake, and then Margaret.

Now it was Frances' turn and my turn.

Frances, drawing back, said, "Un-huh, I'm not going. I'm afraid."

So was I, but I didn't want to admit it. Therefore I stepped back and prepared to leap. "One, two,—!"

Pappy from the barn below, shouted, "Children, no more of that, you are tearing up the strawrick. Go play something else."

That voice saved me from what I was sure would be sudden death, or at the least, from becoming an invalid for life. I certainly didn't share the regrets of the others at having their fun terminated.

Wilbur, with his usual resourcefulness, said, "I know what we can do. There are a coupla' empty barrels over here on the floor; let's roll down the barn hill in 'em."

"That sounds like fun!"

"Let's get 'em!"

Elizabeth shouted, "I'll go first!" as we maneuvered the barrels out onto the barn bridge.

"Elizabeth, you say you wanta' go first?" asked Jake.

"Yeah, I wanta' go first, but you all will have to hold the barrel for me."

So we held it tightly, while she curled around and fitted and wedged herself in as best she could.

Margaret cautioned, "Be sure it's headed down straight before you let it go!"

"I'm ready, let her roll!" yelled Elizabeth.

So we let her roll. The barrel took off down the rough barn hill bumpity bump, bump, bump at considerable speed.

"I'll get in the other barrel!" shouted Jake.

After the experience with one barrel, we knew the technique. So again we let her roll.

96

Elizabeth, on her return to the top with the barrel, stated, "That was great!"

One after another we took our turns rolling down in the barrels and pushing them back up. I must confess, I didn't fully share Elizabeth's enthusiasm that it was great. As the barrel rolled down the rough decline at its dizzy speed, one's head would jolt, then the backbone, the bottom, the knees, the elbows; and with each revolution the process was repeated, until blessed relief as the barrel came to a standstill at the foot of the hill. We certainly worked our guardian angels overtime in this escapade; if perchance one of the barrels had gone off the high rock walls on either side of the barn hill, the results would likely have been disastrous.

At that moment Jasper appeared in the open barn door. "Jake, it looks like we might have a storm afterwhile, so I think you'd better go bring in the cows. Esther, you and Frances run to the house and tell Mother you are goin' with Jake to get 'em. He'll need help since it is earlier than we generally bring 'em in. They won't be at the gate waitin' so you'll have to find 'em and drive 'em in."

Margaret said hurriedly, "Elizabeth, if it looks like rain we'd better be gettin' home."

As predicted, we had to locate the cows when we got to the pasture. We spied them grazing on the hill across the "crick." And as predicted, we had to round them up since they still wanted to graze.

"Soo-ky! Soo-ky! Sooky!" we called over and over as they slowly and reluctantly moved in our direction.

At last as they neared us, we moved behind the herd and drove them, "Huhy! Huhy!"

"Go on move! Huhy!"

"Huhy! Huhy! Huhy!" we yelled, all the way to the gate that opened onto the big road. From thence, our job became easier, as there was little opportunity for grazing and they were confined by the banks and fences on either side.

Frances asked Jake, "Why does that old cow keep tryin' to get up on the back of that other one?"

"Yeah, Jake, you'd better make her get down," I said, adding my bit of advice.

Jake, in a smug all-knowing way, said, "Don't pay any attention to them, just mind your own business," but offered no further elucidation.

It may not seem understandable that even *young* farm girls were not knowledgeable on certain facts of life; but the truth is: it was not thought proper for them to be present at or to observe mating and birthing among animals. Perhaps this was the early puritanical influence on our Dutch cultural and moral life.

The cows were safe in the barnyard and we in the house before the rain came; one of those violent storms that often follows a long, hot, dry spell. The sky grew dark; the house even darker. The kaleidoscopic flashes of lightning snapped in the yard and fields that surrounded us. The thunder reverberated through the house, rattling the windows and doors. The trees dipped and swayed in the driving wind and the tin roof on our house moved in rhythmic undulations. The rain came in torrents obscuring the barn—it seemed no longer there. The cats, the chickens, and all the animal life on the farm scurried for shelter. Our family, too, had found haven in the house, but even so, a storm on a farm can be a very frightening experience; so mother and daughters huddled in the stairsteps between the front room and the parlor which was a bit more secluded from the sights and sounds of the outdoors. But Pappy paced from room to room, from windows to doors, as he habitually did at such a time. Occasionally, he stepped to the dining room porch to glance in the direction of the other farm buildings. There was always the fear of lightning setting fire to the barn, which now held our year's supply of hay and wheat crops.

Finally, the storm passed, and along with its passing our tensions and fears ceased, also. But the rain continued to fall gently and constantly through the evening and into the night. As we lay on our straw ticks, we could hear its rhythmic pitter-patter on the tin roof over us, a part

98

of a symphony of peace, security, and love that permeated our house as we drifted off to sleep.

CHAPTER 7

APPLEBUTTER

"Giddup, Chester! Giddup, Morg!" Jasper ordered the two horses pulling the big wagon along the dusty road. From then on, he periodically slapped them with the lines and made the little clicking sound in his throat that means "move along."

Frances and I sat in the wagon bed flat on our bottoms, feet extended in front of us. Jake stood up beside his older brother, endeavoring to display his manhood. We were on our way to the "newground" beyond the pasture land at the edge of the woods to plow out our winter's supply of potatoes. The morning was young and bright and beautiful. The wind ruffled our hair and billowed out our cotton dresses on "petticoatless" bodies. The clear notes of the meadow lark and the bobwhite sounded across the fields and woods. As we jostled along the rough road down one hill and up the other in the pasture, Frances and I held on to the sides of the wagon as it tilted in one direction and then another. On arrival at the potato patch, we hopped down from the wagon and darted into the woods alongside the newground. We wanted to enjoy the cool shade until Jasper hitched one of the horses to the plow; the respite was all too short.

"Frances and Esther, come on; we're ready now," he called.

The plow sank into the dark brown, loose earth and the potatoes rolled out on each side of the furrow. Buckets in hand, we followed the plow and filled our pails as we moved along. Each time our containers filled, we carried them back and emptied them in sacks that had been placed at the ends of the rows.

The sun became hotter and hotter, the rows grew longer and longer, as Jasper seemed to be plowing each one numberless times. Our hands and barefeet became dry and encrusted with dirt and we were *so* hot and thirsty, but we kept doggedly at the job. We resolved not to leave any potatoes in the furrows. Frances and I even picked up a few of the little marbles that were too small for cooking, except in a playhouse.

Our diligence was not motivated, however, by any overwhelming necessity to reap a large potato crop for the family table through the winter months; but rather, by a promise that Mother had made to us a few days preceding.

She had suggested, "Esther, if we can harvest a good crop of potatoes and beans, and nothing happens to any of my turkeys before market time, maybe we can afford those button shoes you have been wishing for. We'll get each of you a pair."

This incentive was powerful enough to keep me persistently at the hot, dirty, backbreaking job of harvesting potatoes. When finally the last bucket was emptied and Jasper had loaded the sacks onto the wagon, Frances and I climbed aboard with somewhat less alacrity than we had earlier. We sank down among the formless sacks of potatoes. At that moment, it would have been difficult to determine which were more inert, we or the lifeless bags.

"Well, we have a pretty good crop of potatoes even though we had some dry weather a little while back," said Jasper, giving a favorable appraisal of the yield.

At least one ear on my inert body picked up that news.

"Giddup, Chester! Giddup, Morg! Move along, click, click!"

Our hard work of the morning brought another bonus —we were permitted to have most of the afternoon free from further task assignments. Thus I could curl up on the porch swing with my beloved book which was at the time *Daddy Longlegs* by Jean Webster recently borrowed from Frances D.

September was almost ready to push August into yesterday. The goldenrod and Queen Anne's lace had replaced the dandelions and the daisies in the fields and meadows. Weeds and grasses had completed their blooming cycle and were turning dry and seedy. Only a scattering of strawberry red and longstem apples hung here and there on the trees, but the maiden's blush and smokehouse were ripening and inviting us to pluck them. Mother and Pappy decided it was time to accept this challenge and thus it was we soon found ourselves in the middle of applebutter boiling.

Pappy at the back porch, called, "Daughters, get your buckets and come on now, I am ready to get down the apples for cider." The ones to which he was referring were two trees of small sweet apples called agates that were excellent for producing good cider, a major ingredient of applebutter.

Wilbur, Jake, Mary, Frances, and I made a sort of distant ring around the trees as Pappy grasped each limb with a firm hold and gave it a vigorous shake. The apples rained from the tree and covered the ground. As Pappy moved to the second tree to repeat the operation, our work began.

Mary called to Frances, who had plopped on the ground beside her bucket and was trying to fill it from a sitting position, "Get up and get to work, Frances!"

"I am working! You do something yourself!"

"Ow, ow, ow! I stepped on a bee and he stung me! Ow, ow!" I squawked as I hopped around on one foot.

Wilbur fussed, "Gee whiz! You two girls aren't worth nuthin'!" as I, half running, half hopping, started to the house for Mother's medication and consolation.

But while our usual jawing back and forth took place, we somehow proceeded to get the job done, and Pappy tried the fat sacks readying them to load on the wagon.

The morning seemed still yesterday when we arose. At the breakfast table Mother made a proposal. I am sure it was her effort to add interest to the mundane task of applebutter making, which would last for the next two full days. As she passed a sheet of tablet paper around the table, she said, "Each of you sign your name on this paper, and beside it write down the number of gallons of applebutter you think we will make. The one who guesses the nearest to the correct amount will get a prize."

"Hot diggidy! What's the prize?"

"What's the prize?"

"What will we get?"

"Quick, tell us!"

"Monday is court day in town and Pappy will be going in, whoever wins can go along with him and buy a book of their choice," Mother announced.

"Whoopee! I hope I win!"

"I hope I do!"

"Me too! Me too!"

"I wanta' get the book!"

With the scarcity of storybooks or other interesting reading material at our house and no available libraries, Mother could not have suggested an award that would have been more welcome. So we quickly complied by putting our names on the paper and our estimates by them.

Mother continued, "Now whoever wins ought to try and pick a book that everyone can enjoy as far as this is possible."

"We will!"

"We will, we will!"

Going to Harrisonburg on Court Day, or any day for that matter, was a privilege in itself. This was the Monday that court convened, and usually the farmers from the surrounding areas would drive into town. Here they bought and traded; talked about the weather and their crops; discussed the economy of the country and its politics.

For Jake and Wilbur, and Frances and me the anticipation of a trip to town and buying a new book took some of the drudgery out of the chore of picking up the smoke-house and maiden's blush apples for schnitzing.

"I hope I can be the winner. I know what kinda' book I'm goin' to choose," exclaimed Wilbur.

Knowing Wilbur's taste in reading material, I interrupted, "Yeah, I bet you'll choose something about history."

"You're right, Esther, history is my favorite subject."

"I'd choose a good story book or a novel; that's what I like."

Frances, who was still a very young reader, said, "I "I think I'll get the *The Three Bears,* or the *Three Little Pigs,* or maybe just a picture book."

Wilbur scolded, "Aw, Frances, you can't do that. Mother said that it must be something that most of us can enjoy. Who'd wanta' read those silly baby stories?"

As we chatted, buckets were being filled and borne to the house, where Mother and the older girls were already assembling with pans, knives, and tubs into which to throw the schnitz as they were cut. The preparing of the apples extended from early in the morning into the night, when we finished by lamplight. In the meantime, Jasper, with the help of Wilbur and Jake, loaded the cider apples into the wagon along with two empty barrels and drove off to the one and only cider press in the community. Late in the afternoon when they returned, we were more than ready for a break and some refreshment. With a tin cup or two, or three, we lined up by the newly-filled barrels. Pappy slowly and carefully pulled the bung part way from the bung hole letting the sweet fresh cider trickle into our cups. No rule of modern sanitation governed our lives enough to diminish our enjoyment of the sweet juice of the apple in drinking from a common cup.

Pappy arose the next morning ahead of the rest of the family and made a fire under the big, shiny, copper kettle to boil down the cider, the first step in making the applebutter. At the proper minute the tubs of apples were poured into this and their cooking was underway. At that point our work began, for this mixture had to be stirred constantly. Back and forth, and round and round, all the way to the bottom by means of a great long-handled stirrer with an immense wooden paddle on the end—shaped like a giant's long foot with holes at the toe part. Turns to stir came and went on through the morning hours, lunch time, and afternoon. Little tremors of excitement sparked our thoughts and conversations as we wondered and speculated about the number of gallons that would be produced.

This was expressed by the constant queries:

"Isn't it done yet, Mother?"

"When will we dip it up?"

"Don't you think it's thick enough?"

And Mother, with the patience and perseverance we so lacked, would reply, "Not quite yet. We'll have to let it get a little thicker. It won't be too much longer."

In time the long handle was passed to me. I grasped it with both hands, stirring in circles, squares, and isosceles triangles, as my thoughts, too, patterned themselves about in my head—thoughts of going away to school one day; thoughts of what I wanted to be when I grew up—movie actress, missionary, school teacher, nurse. Somewhere in the misty future there appeared a faceless, formless figure of the proverbial Prince Charming. The only certainties about this nebulous being were that he would provide me with an easier life and he would not be a Dutchman. No big kettle of deep red applebutter appeared in my future.

The time came at last when Mother dumped in the sugar and spices that gave it that special fragrance; and we knew that the time for dipping it into the crocks was shortly at hand.

"You children will have to stay out of the way, or I'll never get it dipped into the crocks, and you are liable to get burnt," cautioned Mother.

But as she ladled it into the containers, her warning was scarcely sufficient to keep us from shoving each other in the door in our efforts to watch and count. Finally, she closed us out, while Jasper and Pappy set the filled crocks aside to cool. We were as nervous and fidgety as boys with wheat chaff in their britches from this Motherinflicted suspense. At the point where we thought we could endure it no longer, the door opened again.

"Are you ready?" called Pappy.

Mother teasingly asked, "Are you sure you want to know?"

Pappy, with a twinkle in his blue eyes, said, "Mother, maybe we ought to wait until bedtime to reveal the winner."

"Aw come on, tell us!"

"Please tell us!"

Pappy said laughing, "We made twenty-three and one half gallons. Very good, very good!"

"Oh boy, oh boy! I guessed twenty-three! I won! I won!" shouted Wilbur, bouncing up and down in rhythm with his words.

Bertha, whose arithmetic skill was more advanced than Wilbur's, said, "I guessed twenty-four and that is just as close!"

A little argument over that statement ensued among us with little knowledge of fractions, but was quickly resolved by Mother and Pappy, who often seemed to have Solomon-like resources for finding just solutions.

"Bertha is correct, so this is what we'll do; since we have so many nice apples, we'll take several bushels to town with us. I think we can sell enough so that both Wilbur and Bertha can each select a book."

That took much of the disappointment from the rest of us losers in the contest.

Applebutter making was completed for the fall on the following morning when Mother tied newspapers across the top of each crock with twine, and the boys carried them to the washhouse loft for the hundreds of future applebutter sandwiches that would be found in our school lunch buckets all winter long.

To dispense with the second barrel of cider, we canned some of it while it was still sweet; it was contrary to the precepts of our church and our Pappy to ever allow fermented beverages in his household. The remainder was left in the barrel and carried to the cellar to sour into vinegar for the family supply. No self-sufficient family with apples would permit itself to go into the winter without its own produced supply of vinegar. The family excitement still remained however even after applebutter making was completed. For there was Monday!

And Monday was a long, long day, not by sun-time, but by the measurement of eager impatient children. However, as time has always done, it finally passed, and we saw Pappy, Bertha, and Wilbur drive the buggy in the gate. There was joy that evening in the Pence family over two books that became a part of our limited, dog-eared supply. In time the two new books also grew dog-eared, for Bertha's choice, *The Girl of the Limberlost* by Gene Stratton Porter, became one of our favorites. I should be able to quote some of it verbatim; over the years I read and reread it unrecorded times. Wilbur's book on *General Washington and the American Revolution* may not have been quite as well-loved by the female side of the family, but it too became a well-worn volume.

Two longs and one short rang the bells of the telephone on the wall in the front room. Mary, the first one to it, as frequently happened, shouted, "I'll answer it!" and turned the little handle on the side, signaling the person on the other end to pick up the receiver.

"Hello."

"Is that you, Mary?" asked Frances D.

"Yes, it's me."

"When are you coming down?"

"It's your turn to come up."

"No, it's your turn."

"No, you come."

"You come."

"You come up."

"You come down."

"No, you come."

"You come."

And on and on until Mother interrupted, "Mary, it's time you put down that receiver. Someone else might want the line."

Mary informed Frances, "Mother says I have to hang up now."

"Come down and spend the day with me tomorrow and we'll pop some corn," invited Frances.

"I'll ask Mother. Mother, can I spend the day with Frances tomorrow? She wants me to."

Mother, rejecting Mary's request, said, "No, Mary, tomorrow we are going to the newground and bring in the bunch beans. It will take all of us the whole afternoon to get them shelled. So tell Frances 'no' for this time."

Mary dejectedly obeyed and thus ended that repetitive conversation.

And sure enough as Mother had announced, on the following morning, Jasper, Wilbur, Jake, Frances, and I found ourselves on the same wagon on our way to the same newground where we had been harvesting potatoes a short time before, this time to gather the rows and rows of bunch beans already dried and dying and ready for shelling. We pulled up the entire stalks and tossed them into the big wagon. This was simply another job that farm children must accept, no matter how difficult, as a part of their life in a family that was an economic entity. This time we were jostled home midst stacks of dusty bean vines in place of fat sacks of potatoes. And again we displayed about as much aliveness as the vines surrounding us. With an extra crack or two of the lines and "Giddup! Giddup!" Jasper drove the team of horses up the steep incline of the barn hill and onto the barn floor. With a pitch fork, he rather carefully lifted the beans from the wagon and piled them in a heap on the floor, then backed the wagon out and down the hill. After lunch was over, preparations began for the task awaiting us in the barn.

Mother said, "Esther, run down to Aunt Mags' and see if we can borrow their *Youth's Companion* so that we can read to each other while we are working on the beans. Now don't stay, for we have lots to do."

The *Youth's Companion* was a thin little newspaper-like magazine that was subscribed to by some households in those days.

By the time I returned home with this periodical, the family had already assembled in the barn with dining room chairs on which to sit and pans to use a bit later. Both the front and back barn doors had been opened wide to allow the cool breeze to pass through. We sat in a circle and aimed our beans at a huge basket on the floor, as we pulled them off the vines. While the basket was filling, Ruth began reading the *Youth's Companion* —entertainment as we toiled. We all loved stories—from Mother almost to Frances. The next one on the agenda was a serial, "Eyes that See Not," from *The Grit,* a weekly that Mother and daughters had been reading as each new issue of the paper came. We took turns in the reading aloud, which gave us periodical relief from bean pulling. Even I was given an opportunity to participate, which I did with some aplomb.

"Girls, I think we have read enough for now. Perhaps we'll get our work done a little sooner if we concentrate more on it and less on trying to listen to stories."

After all the bean pods had been pulled from the vines, Pappy and the boys stuffed them in fertilizer sacks and tied them securely. These sacks became real punching bags, as we beat them with boards and stomped them with our feet, turning them over and over in the process. The more we forced them from the hulls by this method, the less we would have to shell by hand afterwards.

Wilbur boasted, as he and Jake expended their energies in beating and stomping, "I'll beat the stuffin's out of this old bag!"

"Don't try too hard, or you might pop it," advised Pappy.

But alas, the pommeling the boys administered did not complete the job; it was necessary to separate the hulls from the beans. So back to the chairs the crew of bean-shellers went.

At that moment, I glanced out the door and spied Elizabeth and Margaret climbing the barn hill. "Hey, Mother, there come Elizabeth and Margaret, can Frances and I go play now? We have company." With that question I set my pan aside and jumped up eagerly and hopefully.

Mother replied, "No, Esther, we are not through yet; you can't leave. Margaret and Elizabeth can come in and sit with us if they want to. Maybe they would like to join us in some singing for awhile."

They did come in and sit, but they were not any more eager to get involved with beans than most farm children. They participated in the singing however, as we sang some of our old favorites.

Margaret suggested, "Cousin Mary, let's sing 'Lilly-O'* all of you know this song so well and I'd like to learn it."

"Lilly-O" was followed by someone else's suggestion of "Charles Guiteau."* Finally Mother and Pappy suggested a hymn or two, as they loved to hear us sing some of their favorites. We complied by singing "I Saw a Wayworn Traveler"* and "Come Unto Me.**

By the time we had finished this last hymn, Margaret and Elizabeth rather quickly made their departure with the invitation, "You all come over soon. How about Sunday afternoon, then we can all go out and play a game?"

At the point of finishing when we were brushing off our dry, dusty, dirty hands, Wilbur jumped up and shouted, "I think it's time to sing 'Hallelujah! Amen!'" with loud emphasis on the "Amen!"

Pappy and the boys carried the freshly-hulled beans outside on the barn hill and poured them slowly from one tub to another, allowing the wind to blow out pieces of hulls, leaves, or any extraneous material left in them. Sometimes we assisted in the winnowing by fanning with hats, papers, or magazines, or whatever was available. Finally they were put into a cloth poke, tied, and stored for this family of bean eaters.

Every completion of a fall chore brought me nearer the moment when I would get my new button shoes, and

---

*Glossary
**The Brethern Hymnal, 1901, 1951.

nearer the day for the fall opening of school. I loved school, as did most of my brothers and sisters. No matter that there was more work than play; that we would go back to drafty rooms heated by the same pot-bellied stoves; that drinks would have to be gotten from the same well pump by the walk; that our toilet was a breezy six-hole outdoor scheishaus; that we had to walk two miles to and from school every day. My anticipation was enhanced by the knowledge that this term I would be in a room upstairs; and thus I would be privileged to march up the broad long flight of stairs and into my room to sit in a single desk, all my own, instead of a double to which I had been accustomed. I truly was growing up at last.

Thus, when Pappy informed us girls that we would now have to blade the cane to get it ready for making molasses, we accepted the announcement with little fuss, albeit with little relish. This was one chore among many that revealed our status as plain, hardworking, farm girls who performed tasks that resulted in sore, rough, calloused hands.

We moved up and down the rows pulling off the blades that cut and scratched our gloveless hands. Pappy followed, decapitating each plant by chopping off the seedy heads. At length, there they stood, a patch of gaunt stiff stalks ready for cutting, then the molasses-making process.

We came to the house, pulling off our hot sunbonnets as we walked and almost literally licking our wounded hands.

Mother met us at the door saying, "Come on in, girls, and I'll put some Raleigh's Salve on your hands."

This salve or ointment Mother purchased from the Raleigh man who peddled his wares periodically over the countryside. The extent of her purchase was usually a bottle of vanilla, one of liniment, and a flat round box of salve. The last two were rather standard first-aid items to be found in most households. Generally there was a number of other items in the peddler's sample case but Mother never bought the frivolous ones, only the necessities. The salve which she now produced from the safe had the looks and smell of carbolated axle grease, but it was soothing to our hands and did have some curative powers.

Mother, from her years of experience, knew how we felt, and added further, "You girls won't have to help with supper or dish washing afterwards. Elizabeth will help me with these things." Elizabeth seldom participated in field and garden work anymore, for she liked to keep soft hands, fair skin, and dainty feet. Elizabeth limited her work to chores of the indoor variety. She was keeping company with a beau, and at that time, looks seemed much more important to courting couples.

The next morning while we were still sleepy, Cousin John Good arrived with his cane press and sorghum boiler, ready to turn cane into molasses. The cane was fed into the rollers of the press which squeezed the juice from the stalks and let it flow into a vat. The rollers were turned by means of a horse hitched to a long pole fastened to them. The horse moved round and round in a well-worn circle as he traced the same path over and over. A fire was made under the vat and the juice was boiled down to a thick brownish syrup—molasses. This was a day-long process, but finally the thick syrup was poured into large lard tins, making one more addition to the family's supply of food for the winter.

Sweet, thick, syrupy molasses seemed to spell taffy—and the making of it seemed to suggest the gathering of neighbors and friends.

Bertha made the plans. "Esther, phone Margaret and Elizabeth and ask if they all can come over for a taffy pullin' this evening, and Mary, you like to talk to Frances. You phone her."

As usual, Mary reached the telephone first. "Frances, can you come up after supper? We wanta' make taffy from our new molasses."

After a pause, Frances replied, "Grandma says I can come."

"Good! Come as soon as you can."

111

"I sure will."

"Goodby."

"Get away, Mary, it's my turn," I broke in trying to push Mary aside.

I cranked out two short rings and my reply came quickly, "Hello!"

"Hello, Elizabeth. We're gonna' make taffy this evening after supper. Can all of you come over?"

Again after a pause, the answer came, "Mother says that we can come. Boy, I can hardly wait! I love taffy!"

"We'll see ya' then. Goodby."

"Goodby."

"They can come! They can come!" I sang out, jumping up and down with excitement.

The kitchen and porch were rocking with activity, as we all gathered there after supper: Bertha, Ruth, Mary, Frances, and I; Frances D., Margaret, Elizabeth, Virginia, and even little Ruth Bowman. The boys were just hanging around the edges making nuisances of themselves. Our sister Elizabeth sat in the front room with Pappy and Mother, busily sewing tatting around the edges of some handkerchiefs. She occasionally looked in at the kitchen door to check on our progress.

The molasses was boiling on the stove in a large skillet, being stirred and tested occasionally to determine its readiness for pulling—not by the modern thermometer method, but by letting it drip from a spoon and observing if it were forming what was known as hairs. The excitement rose in direct ratio to the progress of the boiling contents of the skillet.

Finally, at long last, Bertha shouted, "I think it's ready! Now get outa' my way until I pour it into these buttered pie pans! I don't wanta' burn anybody!"

Allowing it to cool a little, but not wanting it to harden, we each grabbed a wad that was still hot, even to our greased toughened hands. Then began the pulling and folding, back and forth, back and forth. Elizabeth B., observing that Mary and Frances D. had combined their efforts, said, "Esther, let's put ours together."

We stretched the larger hunk into a longer and longer

rope, swinging it back and forth and up and down. It's to be confessed that our concern about whacking the taffy into someone's hair or dropping an occasional lump on the floor wasn't too great. Our accuracy at times, however, was commendable. Frances, with her head of curly hair and participating very little in the pulling, had a habit of darting back and forth under our extended ropes, usually followed by Virginia and Ruth.

Margaret said, "Mine is gettin' so stiff that I can't hardly pull it anymore."

"Mine, too."

"Mine, too. Let's stop. I'm gettin' hungry for some."

From the porch where the boys had been hanging around waiting for the finished product, Jake yelled, "That stuff oughta' be cooked to a frazzle by this time! Maybe you all are eatin' every bit of it up like pigs!"

We twisted our molasses ropes and coiled them around in the pie pans like snakes ready to strike. Ruth and Bertha then marked them off in regular blocks to be broken off in pieces for eating. We sucked and chewed the tough sweet lumps of taffy with gusto. Temporarily this put a limit on the level of chatter; nothing had to be said to express our joy of the moment.

Ruth volunteered, "I'll take some in to Mother and Pappy and Elizabeth," as she dashed off with a panful.

Wilbur and Jake were busily chewing as they stood on the porch to catch the pleasant breeze. I joined them to also get a breath of fresh air away from the heat produced by the stove and the other little generators milling about the kitchen. Wilbur, with a baseball pitcher's wad in his cheek, bragged, "How do you like my 'terbaccer'?" And he spat a globule of brown juice out into the yard in front of him.

Jake jeered, "Aw, I bet I can spit my 'terbaccer' farther'n you can."

Wilbur took the challenge. "Wanta' bet?" And with that he shot the umber liquid, with a quick, jerky, little squirt, about ten feet in front of him. "Jake, I bet ya' can't beat that."

Jake yelled, "Watch this!" as he put all his force into his spew.

Wilbur argued, "My 'spectorant went farther'n yours."

As they continued their spitting, when they could produce the necessary saliva, I watched with envy and fascination. For a long time, I had wanted to squirt and spit like that, and I had tried often after watching the men in the neighborhood, standing around in groups frequently expectorating in this fashion, especially "Old Mr. Bailey" who could spit on a walnut six feet away. So I stepped aside, unnoticed, and again tried, but always with the same results. To this day, I do not know whether my spit lacked the right ingredients, or if I were the wrong sex, for I never did achieve my noteworthy ambition.

"Mother! Frances has a wad of taffy in her hair!"

Mother exclaimed, *"Ach du liewe zeit!** Frances, come here and let me look! This is a mess! I'll just have to cut out a bunch of hair. I don't think you children ever made taffy without someone getting it in her hair!"

As we went to bed that night, our tummies were puddles of sweet brown syrup, but we were oblivious to the bubbles and gurgles therein as we slept the sleep of the young who have just had a happy experience.

Every day now seemed a bit cooler, as fall began to move in, and the school bell was about to ring. The day came when Mother told Frances and me to take off our "hoodly" (messy) clothes and put on clean ones, for we were going to the store to get our new shoes and some gingham for dresses. I was as bouncy and excited as a skillet of popcorn from that moment until we walked into Yager's Store. The pot-bellied stove already had a small fire to take the bite from the chilly autumn breeze. Our bare feet ran across the oiled floor to find warmth by the familiar stove. On one side of this rather high, spacious room were shelves of spices, soda, baking powder, tobacco twists, plugs, snuff, and sundry items. On the counter, there was a glass candy case and jars of

---

*My goodness! or My gracious!

114

pink and white lozenges, licorice, and horehound candies. There were barrels of sugar—both white and brown, and barrels of crackers, pickles, salt, and flour; nothing was pre-packaged. On the opposite side of the room could be seen a spool drawer, shelves of gingham and calico, unbleached muslin, outing, canton flannel, dark blue denim, and a few bolts of silks and satin. There were a few notions, such as buttons, lace, ribbons, and velvet. Here, too, could be found boxes of long underwear and overalls. Our first interest, however, was to go into the side room where Mr. Yager stocked his shoes.

Mother said, "I told the girls that they could have button shoes this time."

Mr. Yager looked sad. "Mrs. Pence, I'm terrible sorry, but I don't have any children's button shoes left—only a couple pairs of ladies' sizes. They only sent me a few pairs of children's shoes this fall, and I've sold all of them."

Mother looked downcast. "I am sorry, too; the girls had their hearts set on button shoes this time."

I knew that Mother meant this sincerely and that her heart ached, too, at this poignant moment; but that didn't prevent my tears from flowing as Mr. Yager brought out the same old rough rawhide shoes that resembled the ones boys wore, and which I had come to hate.

After we were properly fitted, I thought in desperation, "How could Mr. Yager have so many sizes in these ugly old shoes and almost none of the pretty ones that button!" At that moment I was beyond all ability to reason, so I was just miserably silent.

"Come on, girls, let's go now and choose some gingham for dresses; and my bill probably won't be too high since we had to take the cheaper shoes, so maybe we can get each of you two new hair ribbons to go with your dresses."

We wore our hair bobbed, save for a long plait on the tops of our heads. For everyday wear, this braid was looped under and tied with a string, but on special occasions we wore a large bow of ribbon atop it. We moved to the dry goods shelves, where Frances and I looked over the bolts of material; then after a little whispering between us, we made our decisions: a red checkered piece and a blue checkered piece. Mr. Yager could manage to reach our choices only by climbing a ladder which was fastened to shelves by means of rollers at the top and bottom, and which moved laterally. After taking down the specified bolts of goods and cutting off the required amounts, we chose our ribbons—a red one and a blue one, marked with a wavy watery design.

When all the purchases were made, Mr. Yager, who was conscious of the disappointment that he had caused us, returned to the other side of the store and called, "Come here, girls."

We went, wondering what was going to happen.

"Each of you can have two sticks of candy of your choice."

We selected red and white striped peppermint sticks and green and pink ones flavored with sweet anise.

I suppose we did not camoflage our disappointment very well, for even our pesky brothers taunted us very little when we returned home. Sometimes saying nothing is an act of sympathy, especially when the silence is kept by two usually-teasing boys.

CHAPTER 8

BELSNICKELS

The school bell rang at nine. We lined up double file on the walk leading to our two-story frame building with its inevitable front porch, and marched into the sound of dum-dum, dumdumdum, dum-dum, dumdumdum from the principal's drum. As I walked up the broad steps to the second floor and into my classroom, I felt very pleased with my appearance, from the flouncy, red ribbon bow on my head to the tops of my shoes, where my pride stopped. I could only look upon those shoes as the one flaw in an otherwise pretty outfit.

I chose my new single desk with some pride and care at the front of one row, albeit I did enjoy the back of the room where I could whisper and play on occasions; but to a greater degree I preferred to sit where I could see and participate. While the roll was being called with the responses of "Present," "Present," "Present," I suddenly became aware of the most beautiful pair of button shoes under the desk across the aisle from me. 'Twas then I broke the tenth commandment, for I coveted. Oh, how I coveted those button shoes! I automatically kept my feet down under me as closely as possible—through classes on the long recitation bench at the front of the room, at the blackboard doing my sums (impossible), in my own desk, or at lunch period when friends huddled together. Like "Willie Waddle" who was ashamed of his big feet and hid them, I was ashamed of my ugly feet, so I hid mine.

With the fall opening of school, changes took place in our family. Elizabeth left home to resume her teaching, and Bertha had gone to the Academy at Bridgewater to continue her education, as the local school had no more to offer her. How we missed the hands to help us with those farm chores! Especially we missed Bertha's merriment and jolly good fun and Elizabeth's gentle nature. But their attachment to their family brought them home frequently, to our delight, and Thanksgiving and Christmas vacations found them at home for extended stays.

We happily anticipated the coming of all holidays: Thanksgiving, Easter, Valentine's Day, and Christmas especially, even though our plans and celebrations were simple and uncomplicated.

By Thanksgiving it was quite cold, just as we had hoped. That was our special time for butchering each year, and the temperature needed to be low enough to properly cool the meat for curing. On Thanksgiving, we commemorated the Day with a rare treat—Chesapeake Bay Oysters. It was the one time in the year that oysters were served on our table. Pappy had ordered a gallon several days earlier from the Tilghman Company in Baltimore.

Very early in Friday's cold dawn, the slaughtering of our six hogs began. Otis Bowman, the father of our friends and the neighborhood butcher, was there at 6:30. The fire had already been made under the trough of water in which the pigs would be scalded. This must be the right temperature, for if it were not hot enough, the bristles would not come off; but if it were too hot, then the skin would come off with the bristles. As there were no thermometers for recording the temperature, and no stop watches to accurately time the dunking period, the testing of the water temperature was done by rapidly swishing the hands back and forth through it a time or two. After proper dunking, the carcass was scraped to remove the bristles, then hung on a tall wooden tripod by its hind hegs. From this position the head was cut off, the internal organs removed, and the cutting of the hams, shoulders, and sides followed. By that time, Mother and we girls began to cut up the fat into cubes for lard making. These cubes were thrown into a large iron kettle over the fire in the washhouse where the lard would be fried from them. We ground the sausage meat and seasoned it with red and black pepper, salt, and sometimes coriander. Some of the sausage we pressed into cleaned entrails, which were the only casings we had for stuffed sausage then. Following this, the meat for grinding into pudding was cooked, and the broth from this was used for panhaus. The panhaus was one of our favorite end products of butchering. It was made by taking the juice of the cooked pudding meat and adding cornmeal to it; then this was cooked until it was quite thick. We then poured it into molds to cool. We would later slice this and fry it until it was crisp, and brown, and crunchy.

The lard was rendered by running the fat through a press after the grease had sufficiently fried out. We ground the cooked pudding meat, seasoned it, and poured it into the kettle over the fire to fry out some of the grease, stirring it constantly to keep it from burning. At the finish of this cooking we dipped it into crocks for later serving as puddin' with hominy. Crocks were filled with sausage meat that had been previously prepared.

At about that point, Jake with his hands behind him, came sneaking out of the house.

Mother, never lacking in awareness of what her sons and daughters were up to, and knowing that we often had some practical trickstering in mind, called to him, "Jake, are you slipping pins out of my bureau drawer? You know we don't have many of those to waste."

Jake gave a sort of mumbly answer, "I didn't get but a couple. Wilbur told me to get 'em."

Mother replied, "If anyone gets a tail pinned on him, it oughta' be you two boys, for the way you can eat, you rate pigtails more than anyone else."

It seemed to be a ritual that went with butchering that a pigtail be pinned to the coattails of an unsuspecting victim and provide laughs for all the others. The curliest pigtail was chosen, a straight pin was forced through it, and then bent to form a hook to hang onto the innocent bystander's dress or coattail. It generally took the finesse of a pickpocket to accomplish this. As the afternoon waned, and after several unsuccessful attempts at victimizing Mary, their attentions turned to Frances and me. Their accomplishments at this were usually cut short, as the whispering, snickering, giggling, and finger pointing of the others served to warn us of what was happening. It was our turn to giggle when butchershop closing time came, as Wilbur and Jake, with their moderate success in pigtail pinning, came strutting into the kitchen. When Wilbur unsuspectingly bent over the table for a hunk of newly cooked liver, the snickers and giggles turned into haw-haws, for as this tale ended, the tail was suspended on Wilbur's coattail, and he has never known until this day that the perpetrator of this deed was Otis Bowman, our butcher. No part of the pig was unusable.

Mother finally said, "It's time to get shut (rid) of that thing now for it has served its usefulness."

By late evening all the work had been completed, and the menfolk had trimmed and shaped the hams. If the quantities of the produce were any indication, we had a slaughterhouse for a day on our farm. The men finally cleaned up outdoors, and we had all the greasy equipment inside to wash, which in itself was no small job.

Parts of the process of butchering always carried over into the second day, for the sausage had to be processed by heating in crocks, and the hams, shoulder, and sides had to be cured. Finally, all the finished products—the pudding, sausage, lard, plus the cured meat—were carried to their storage place on the washhouse loft. The cellar and this loft were the family's food market for the year.

For us, our little Christmas generated as much excitement and joy as all the glitter of myriad lights on streets and trees, all the array of toys and gadgets that move, and all the false department store Santa Clauses bring to today's youngsters.

I have never quite figured out when Mother and Pappy bought the limited amount of Christmas they could afford, when they smuggled it into the house, and where they concealed it, with so many hands and eyes in the household exploring every corner and crevice. But come Christmas Eve, they were ready. Mother directed, "Children, put plates at your places at the table and then take yourselves off to bed." No accompanying instruction "go to sleep" was included, for she knew full well there would be a period of wakefulness and excitement, in which we would whisper and giggle about what the next day would have on plates for us.

Pell-mell down the back stairs we dashed on Christmas morning, past the dining table, and into the living room to scramble into our clothes. We consumed very little time on this day to smooth out the lumps from our long underwear as we stuffed them hastily into our stockings. We were just as eager to get Christmas as if there were a tree full of shining ornaments with presents piled high beneath it. So we gathered around the table, each at his own special plate, which contained some pieces of hard candy, a bunch of raisins still on their stems, a few peanuts, and an orange, plus each one's own unique little gift.

Wilbur and Jake, anticipating, exclaimed, "We are goin' outdoors to whittle with our new jackknives!"

Pappy advised, "Be careful what you whittle, sons; be especially sure it isn't your fingers."

Frances and I, laughing, shouted, "As soon as breakfast is over, we are goin' to find some paper and color with our crayons!"

Bertha, Ruth, Mary, and Elizabeth, admiring their little cup and saucer sets, enthused, "I think mine is the prettiest!"

"I like mine because it's blue!"

"I'm goin' to start my hope chest with mine!"

Jasper and Charlie stood happily examining their new pairs of brown knit gloves that would keep their fingers warm on cold wintry days.

In the meantime, Elizabeth had slipped unnoticed out of the room, and at that moment returned with a box which she immediately opened.

"Hershey Bars! Boy, oh boy!"

"I love Hershey Bars!"

"Thank you, Elizabeth, thank you!" echoed over and over.

Elizabeth smiled, "This is my Christmas for everyone. Why don't we let Mother and Pappy have theirs first—you know they didn't get anything else."

As far back in time as I can remember, Mother and Pappy never bought themselves or each other gifts for Christmas. Their joy was made full by the sparkle in the eyes and the excitement from the lips of their children.

Our Christmas dinner consisted of turkey with all the farm-produced trimmings. This was the day on which we ate the one turkey, saved for family consumption, from the flock. The other turkeys had been sold to help buy the necessities of life on the farm.

On Christmas evening, the snow fell gently, silently to bless our house—a haven for a family that knew the joy which came from little things that love provided.

A night or two after Christmas, the first belsnicklers appeared in the neighborhood and made the rounds, including our house. They came in groups of fours, sixes, and tens, wearing well-worn clothing. Quite often the women were dressed in men's outfits and vice versa. They had lisle stockings or cloth sugar pokes pulled down over their faces to hide their identities. And to remain anonymous, they spoke very little except in well-disguised voices. Their actions said more than their words, as they milled about the room with waggish actions, trying to pull tricks on the members of the family. After we had identified most of them, which was not too difficult— they were generally friends and neighbors—they took off their false faces and were served refreshments. These offerings were quite often a big bowl of apples or popcorn.

Belsnickeling was a custom that had its roots among the Pennsylvania Dutch with many variations in practice there and from there to here.

The coming of belsnicklers into our home inspired us to take our turn at belsnickeling also, so it was on the following day that we got on our much-used line to the Bowmans and Frances D. and planned our get-together for the upcoming night. We hunted up old clothes, in some instances stuffing them with pillows to make them fit. We made our masks by cutting eyes, noses, and mouths in old lisle stockings or sugar pokes. Shortly after supper the Bowmans and Frances D. came by in the big sleigh, and we piled in "rootshing" down as far as possible in the straw, and sailed off in the frozen night air.

Jingle bells, Jingle bells, Jingle all the way,

Joy to the world; The Lord has come,
Let earth receive her king.

The Istmas, Listmas, Christmas man,
The Rollicky, Frollicky, Jollicky man.

Silent night, Holy night;
All is calm, all is bright;

We sang carols into the night.

"Gee, my nose is gettin' cold and it keeps on runnin'," interrupted Elizabeth B.

"Yeah, and the snot freezes on my false face," responded Jake.

Frances D. laughed. "This ole' stocking feels kinda' good; it helps keep my face warm. It's so cold tonight."

Our Frances replied, "Yeah, this sugar poke helps keep me warm, too, but I can't find my nose hole, and I can't hardly breathe."

Margaret shivered. "Father, are we goin' by that ole' deserted Brown house? I hope not, 'cause some people say it's haunted and it skeers me!"

Bertha sat up. "Of course we're goin' by it; but why are you scared? There are no such things as haunts and ghosts!"

Elizabeth scrootched down in the seat and she said positively, "There is, too! Somebody told us that one dark night they saw a light movin' from window to window when they passed by that place!"

Frances D. shuddered. "Yeah, and someone else said they saw white things flyin' around there and heard the weirdest noises! They said they were so scared they really ran!"

"Probably was nothing but a ole' Screech Owl they heard," joked Wilbur.

Virginia's little voice spoke up from way down in the seat. "Anyway, I don't care what you say! I don't like that ole' house! Can't you drive faster, Father?"

In spite of all our pretense of bravery, we, too, were glad for him to drive the horses a little faster, while we scrunched down a bit deeper in the hay, and cast only furtive glances in the direction of the haunted house.

We stopped at homes on our route, with generally not

too well camouflaged disguises and not too clever attempts at buffoonery. The offers of refreshments were always gratefully accepted. As we circled and returned home, we met other night spooks on the road and in houses on the same clownish missions. At such times, we mingled with the other crowds in general confusion.

At length the sleigh pulled up to our front gate and we hopped out with cries of: "Thank you," "Good-by," "We had fun," "Goodnight," and "Come over soon!"

Wilbur, as we jumped, yelled, "Jake, where's my apple you stuck in your pocket? Jake! Hey, where is Jake?"

Ruth spoke. "Jake, where are you? I wonder if we left him somewhere! If we did, somebody will have to go after him!"

"I know he was with us at the Longs'. So he must be there," said Bertha.

"I'll bet Mother and Pappy won't let us go belsnickeling again," wailed Mary.

Our apprehension to enter the house at this moment was exceeded only by our desire to come in from the cold; so rather subdued, we walked in. And there sat Jake, already uncostumed and warming by the stove!

Bertha, glad to see him but a little disgusted, said, "For goodness sake, where did you come from?"

Jake mimicked her tone. "Yeah, where *did* I come from? You all went and left me at the Longs'. The Saufleys brought me home; they were comin' here anyway."

Pappy mildly reproved, "If you children can't look after each other any better than that, we'll just have to put a stop to your going belsnickeling."

Rather subdued and sheepish, we shed our costumes, warmed by the fire a few minutes, and took ourselves to bed.

Fortunately, or so we youngsters thought, the snow remained through the holidays, and we "messed around" in it at every opportunity.

Mother, addressing Wilbur and Jake the next morning as they appeared in the kitchen door, said, "Boys, your shoes are soppin' wet from the snow; you'll be sick if you wear those wet things too long. Take them off now, and put them in the little warmer under the oven to dry. Don't shut the door on them, or they will dry out too quickly and get hard."

The little warmer that Mother referred to was a compartment approximately six inches high between the big baking oven and the floor. It probably was there for safety as well as for utilitarian purposes, since those early ranges were without legs and sat flat on the floor.

The boys followed Mother's instructions. Later in the afternoon they went to the kitchen, retrieved their shoes, and shut the little warmer door.

Jake sniffed the air. "Boy! This bread Mother is bakin' smells good! It makes me hungry!"

And Wilbur added contentedly, "Yeah, and this ole' hot fire feels good, too. It sure is cold outside!"

The stove required heavier firing for bread baking and the heat added to the comfort of the house on an almost zero day.

Sometime later, Mother, who was busy with the patching and darning in her lap, suggested to Bertha, "Maybe you had better check on the bread in the oven; and girls, it's about time to start supper. The men will be in soon, and they'll be hungry. Since it's so cold, they decided to finish their work early."

Bertha laid aside her crocheting and started to the kitchen, followed by Ruth and Mary. "Phew!" exclaimed Bertha. "What's that awful smell?"

Ruth and Mary held their noses. "Phew! Phew! That's terrible!"

"Mother! Something smells awful out here! We can't stand it! Come quick!" With that everyone rushed to the kitchen.

"What on earth can it be?"

"It smells like something dead!"

"It smells like the pig pen!"

"It smells like rotten meat!"

"Phew! Phew!"

The odor seemed to be concentrated in the stove area, so Mother lifted the lid off the fire box. She sniffed—

no odor there; she checked the pots and pans—nothing in them.

Finally, Jasper, after sniffing further, opened the little warmer door under the oven where Jake and Wilbur had dried their shoes. The source of the odor was found, absolutely no doubt about it! There are no smell adjectives to adequately describe that odor. But the fumes emanating from that little warmer reeked of the stench of dirt, hair, flesh, and excretion cooking in a cauldron. Looking down, Jasper beheld the tip of Old Tom Cat's tail. He reached in, grabbed that tail, and quickly pulled him out. Poor Old Tom! His fur was wringing wet and clinging together in little bunches, his body was dehydrated from the heat and he was panting for his last breath.

"That smell makes me wanta' vomit!"

"It makes me feel like puking, too!"

Jasper again grabbed him by his tail and flung him out on the back porch into the cold. There was no other alternative.

Frances, who loved Old Tom and who played with him more than anyone else, began to cry, "I don't want Tom to die! Is he dead, Pappy?"

Pappy sympathized, "It looks like it, daughter, but don't cry, for all animals have to die sometime, and I guess Tom's time has come."

None of us felt too much like eating as we sat at the supper table, with some of the foul odor still in the room, and thoughts of our old pet in our minds. While we were sitting quietly trying to consume our food, we suddenly became aware of a queer noise at the dining room door nearest to Jasper and Pappy, and everyone looked up questioningly.

"What's that strange noise?" asked Mary.

Charlie put in, "It sounds like somethin' scrarchin' at the door."

Jasper reached over and opened the door. There in all his usual health, vigor, and appearance, stood Old Tom. With a "meow," he nonchalantly strolled into the dining room, unaware that he had just used up one of his nine lives.

Roses are red, Violets are blue;
Sugar is sweet, And so are you.

I was prepared for my next class recitation, so I sat busily copying, in my best handwriting, verses on valentines I was making for my friends. I had folded sheets of tablet paper in half and then made hearts on one side which I cut around and lifted like little doors. It was under these I was writing my verses:

As sure as the grass grows round the stump,
You are my darling sugar lump.
If you love me, as I love you,
No knife could cut our love in two.

Molasses in the gourd,
Sugar in the cup,
If you aren't a sweet girl
I'll give it up!

Sugar's sweet, butter's greasy,
I love you, so don't be uneasy.

As each fastidious creation was completed, I stacked it in my desk to distribute to my best girl friends, and maybe, to a boy or two who had won my favor—or at least my approval. But I sure wasn't going to give any to that Tommy Crow who called me a "Dumb Dutchman." He always acted so "biggity" and "snobby."

At that moment my reveries and activities were interrupted by teacher calling us to get our primers of hygiene and come to class. We sat on the long recitation bench at the front of the room, reading, discussing, and answering questions. On this day, a part of our lesson concerned the construction of outdoor toilets, which were more numerous in those years than the indoor variety.

In the midst of our discussion and reading, Jake suddenly inquired, "Teacher, what's a sanitary pit privy?"

At that period of time there was a sort of taboo against people speaking openly about such items as toilets and related subjects; so with a sort of embarrassed half laugh, she answered, "Well, Jacob—uh—it's a toilet."

Giggles all along the recitation bench were rather quickly suppressed by a threatening look.

By the time Valentine's Day came, I was ready, for I had a sufficient number of valentines to exchange with my friends and a few to slip into certain acceptable boys' desks. Within me, there had not yet developed any boy-girl feelings, so if there were any demonstrated interest in the opposite sex, it was an attitude more caught than felt—caught from observation of older boys and girls or brothers and sisters. Boys were merely people to be liked or disliked. Cupid's dart had not yet found its mark in my heart, and Valentine's Day did not signify Eros.

CHAPTER 9

DANDELION GREENS

The taste, the feel, the smell of our classrooms were different now. The windows were open and the fresh spring air had chased away the odors of ashes and coal from the pot-bellied stoves, the dust of erasers and blackboards, the smell of human bodies and feet and wornout leather shoes.

The end of school was almost here. Our pencils were mostly little nubs with erasers used up or chewed off; books were dog-eared; and tablets were expended. In the hall, boots and rubbers no longer dripped mud and snow on the floor; and coats had disappeared from their accustomed pegs.

The road home had a changed appearance also; the ruts, deep and muddy in winter, were now flat and dusty, worn down by natural spring erosion and the tramping, kicking feet of school children.

Into the house we clattered, unloading book satchels and lunch buckets on the dining room table; and sweaters, caps, and jackets on the chairs; or in our haste to exit, perchance on the floor.

As I was about to depart, Mother caught me by my intentions, "Esther, I want you to go with Ruth and help her find some dandelion greens for supper."

I wasn't exactly happy at having my own plans thwarted, but then I thought, "Hunting dandelions with Ruth wouldn't be too bad a job, for we could roam the field and talk big girl talk."

Most of the family were quite fond of dandelion which was prepared by chopping it fine, and over this pouring a hot dressing. It's a more tasteful way of getting one's necessary iron supply than any chef's method of glorifying spinach. So with bucket and knives, we went to the field behind the house and began looking for the new tender young plants. Our purposes for starting early in the season were twofold: the leaves were more edible early in the spring before it began to bud and its bright yellow blossoms appeared; also, we were in running competition with our neighbors to have the first mess of dandelion of the season. Each time we located a stalk, we cut it off at the root and tossed it into our bucket.

Ruth, opening our chatter, said, "Esther, did you know that I am goin' to the academy at Bridgewater with Bertha next fall? I sure am lookin' forward to it."

"Won't that be nice for you! What are you goin' to study?"

"I'm goin' to study to be a teacher, just like Elizabeth and Bertha."

Occupational opportunities for girls were quite limited in those days; we had no Women's Lib going for us.

"I sure hope I can go away to school sometime, too. I wanta' study to be something."

"You will when the time comes. I'll have to do some sewin' this summer and get some dresses and underwear made."

"Will you have to wear long drawers at school? I sure hate those things."

"No, we won't need them since we won't be walkin' to school and workin' outdoors so much."

"Gee! I can't hardly wait until I can go." Then, changing the conversation, I said, "Ruth, I sure did get mad at that old Tommy Crow at school today."

"What happened?"

"Well, Elizabeth B. and I were talkin' and I told her we were goin' to try to find some dandelion this evening and Tommy was snootin' in as usual. He said that only Dumb Dutchmen would eat dandelion, 'cause it was cow's food. I told him he was dumber than a cow, 'cause a cow knows what's good."

"Esther, you shouldn't pay any attention to that kinda' talk. It doesn't bother me that I am Dutch. Lots of my friends are Dutch, our church is Dutch, so don't think anything about it."

With that, we started for the house, as we had filled our bucket.

After supper was over, Mary said, "We should phone the neighbors and tell them we had our first mess of dandelion this evening."

"Yeah, I'll phone Elizabeth. I told her at school today we were goin' to try and find some."

After ringing two shorts and getting Elizabeth to the telephone, "Hello, what ya' doin'?"

Elizabeth, on the other end, "I'm not doin' much of anything."

"I'm not doin' much either, now. We just finished our supper and we had our dandelion."

Elizabeth said again, "You lucky thing. We haven't had any yet."

"You say you didn't have any? I'll bet we had the first mess this year."

At that point Aunt Emma, who was listening in on our conversation, chimed in, "No, you're not. We had some yesterday, so we beat you."

In those days party lines, including from six to ten families, served as a medium of exchange of community news. This was especially important in the absence of radio and television newscasts. When a party was being called by a code ring all telephones on the line sounded, thus all parties knew who was being called and were alerted by a short answering ring that the call had been received. Neighbors often lifted receivers and listened, with some even joining the conversation.

At the end of this interruption I said, "I'd better hang up now and study my lessons. I'll see ya' tomorrow, Elizabeth. Goodbye."

Leaving the telephone disgustedly I said, "Well, Aunt Emma busted in on our conversation and said they had dandelion yesterday. I'll bet she'd say that if they didn't have but a teacup full."

"Now, Esther, it isn't nice to talk about your Aunt Emma like that. Don't speak so quickly; children have to learn to control their tongues. You are growing up now; you must have grown a couple inches taller this winter, so try to grow in your behavior too."

As I looked down at my long feet, I replied, "Yeah, my feet grew a couple inches too; they have just about poked the ends out of these old ugly shoes; and I don't care a bit."

In the days ahead, we not only gathered dandelion and ate it, but we hunted for dry land cress, and mixed greens of broad leaf plantain, narrow leaf dock, mouse ear cress, and lamb's quarter—a welcome infusion of greens to our diets.

Another source that provided variety in our diet was a fish trap. This trap was a neighborhood endeavor which the farmers had designed, engineered, and built across the river to catch the fish as they swam downstream. Each family participant in the project had an assigned night to collect the fish thus caught, which might include: sun perch, suckers, eels, and an occasional bass. Also, there were times when the river was swollen after heavy rains that the boys went dipping with the big dip net, and would bring home a nice catch. Generally, the fish trap and dipping net gave us fish in larger supply than a line and hook—all this was before laws against these methods; and when farmers were not sportsmen, but men providing the food supply for their families.

"Elizabeth is coming! Elizabeth is coming!" shouted Frances, as she jumped off the palings in the front yard and ran around to the back of the house.

Summer vacation was beginning for us, even though it was only the first of May—school was out and Elizabeth was coming home from her winter of teaching. Each newborn day seemed to bring an assortment of events and activities as life surged in the fields, meadows, and farm buildings around us.

Frances and I were hunched on our knees, hovering over a basket of newly hatched baby turkeys that Mother had placed behind the cook stove. They were still wobbly and wet; and the warmth from the stove would help dry their down. They occasionally flapped their wings and moved their bodies to assist this drying process. When their down dried and fluffed, they were so cunning that Frances and I could hardly keep our hands off them; but Mother restrained us partially by an occasional warning: "Girls, don't handle them too much, that is not good for little turkeys."

Turkeys, too, meant shoes and coats and underwear for the family.

Mother said again, "Esther, come now and take some feed and water to the little chickens."

In the weeks preceding whenever we observed hens ready for setting, Mother would provide them with a nest of fifteen eggs in a somewhat secluded part of the henhouse. They indicated their desires to become mothers by refusing to leave their nests and by frequently making funny little clucking sounds as if already mothering a brood of baby chicks. When we placed water and feed near them during this three-week incubation period, we had the opportunity to observe the protective instincts of animals; usually from afar, because they were fussier than normally at this period and were inclined to pick one with their sharp beaks. The setter would periodically turn over her eggs with her feet or beak; and then gently sit down on them again, fluffing out her feathers to cover and protect the entire nestful.

At the end of the three weeks, we observed that the eggs were being picked and cracked by the forces of new life within; and the hen's mothering instincts were completely satisfied when she was placed in an individual coop with her babies—a truly happy family. No condominiums, no apartments, no ghettos—just one-family units.

By this time, we had several of these one-family units in their coops in the chicken yard. To these, as Mother had instructed, I went with a pan of cracked corn and threw a couple handfuls in each coop while the mother hen clucked her flock to the table. I followed this with water, pouring some in each low can top container; low so the babies could drink from it; shallow so they would not fall in deep water and drown.

Finally, setting my pans down, I walked along the path a few yards farther to the scheïshaus, where I decided to sit and read for awhile. With the old newspapers, magazines, and catalogs, we had a fair supply of reading material; and sometimes the most private place on our farm was the privy. By now, reading was my favorite pastime; I consumed romances, stories, and novels, with the fervor of an addict.

On my return from this sanctuary, I again came by the chicken coops, retrieved my feed and water pans, and dropped them quickly and quietly on the kitchen porch. From thence, I slipped around the house, rather than passing through, recovered my current novel, *The Girl of the Limberlost*, from the swing, opened it, and was soon chasing butterflies and moths in the Limberlost. My attention was diverted only by an occasional fly that zoomed around my head, or lit on my bare feet and legs; or the scraping of Pappy's shovel as he scooped up the manure in the big road, dropped there by horses and cows, and tossed it over the fence into the field. Pappy had a conviction that he should use all forms and quantities of fertilizer to enrich the soil; none should be wasted. He also held a concern for the appearance of his farm and its surroundings.

By afternoon, I decided on another spot to maintain my privacy, as the front porch, by that time, would be quite warm from the rays of the afternoon sun. I thought myself into believing that if I went into the parlor and hid behind the organ, no one could find me; I would avoid hearing their calls. Our parlor was used only when my sisters' fellows called or Sunday company came, so the shades behind the straight lace curtains were kept drawn through the week. As I entered this haven, it was cool, quiet, and inviting. The red and green flowered rug on the floor felt soft to my bare feet. The chairs and settee with their overstuffed seats were stiff, prim, and uncomfortable.

On the wall to my left hung a gilt-framed picture of Saint Cecilia in her soft crimson robe draped over an azure blue dress, playing the harpsichord. Her saintly face gazed heavenward to a cluster of cherubic angels in an ethereal mist. Across from her on the opposite wall was Mother and Pappy's wedding certificate, decorated with flowers and white-robed angels and signifying that Samuel Pence and Mary Harshbarger were united in marriage on the 2 day of April, A. D. 1891. Over the fireplace hung Grandmother Harshbarger's portrait in her little black cape and Dunker prayer cap tied under her chin.

I sat down on the floor in the corner by the organ farthest from the door, and soon was wandering once more in the Limberlost. Sometime and somewhere in the distance I vaguely heard family conversations: Frances calling, "Where's Esther? I want her to play with me. Esther!"

Mother remarking, "I don't think Esther did a very good job of brushing crumbs out of the dining room."

I turned them off and continued reading.

134

It was unheard of to wash any day but Monday, and this was Monday. Jasper made a fire under the iron kettle in the washhouse, while Frances and I pumped soft rain water from the cistern to fill it. After breakfast was over and the water was heated, washday on the farm began: a tub of warm water, a scrub board, homemade soap, a kettle of boiling water for scalding clothes, two tubs of rinse water (the final one with bluing added), a human hand-wringer; sore knuckles and fingers, chapped hands, tired backs, aching legs and feet—at last, lines of clothes, a week's supply of clean laundry. Today's wash was one of those sometimes extra large ones that required extra line space, so we threw the surplus pieces over the field and yard fences.

Mother called from the kitchen, "Esther, tell the girls not to empty the wash water until you and Frances wash the porches and walks."

We frequently used the sudsy water for this purpose, following it with the rinse water. "Make use of what you have and don't waste anything," was Mother's and Pappy's motto.

When washday ended, everyone was ready for rest. By the time I had found something to read, the family had already assembled in the living room for the night; all chairs being occupied, including those from the dining room.

"Mother, where can I sit? I don't have a chair."

Wilbur teased, "Sit on your fist and lean back on your thumb."

Mother, ignoring Wilbur's remark, ordered, "Girls, move closer together there on the couch and make room for Esther. It's about bedtime anyway."

Thus we settled down for the night.

"There comes Mr. Burgess! I'll get the mail! I'll get the mail!" shouted Mary as she dashed for the mailbox by the front gate.

Mr. Burgess approached in his sports model buggy, with its folded-down top, pulled by a dapple gray horse. As he drew in the reins and came to a stop, he put our daily mail, which he had previously sorted out, into Mary's outstretched hands.

"I see you have a letter from Grace today," he said, indicating an interest of neighbor for neighbor, which could not be categorized as nosiness.

Mary retraced her steps around the house and called, "We got a letter from Grace! We got a letter from Grace!"

She handed the letter to Mother who quickly opened and read it.

"Grace is coming home this summer for a few weeks. I'm so grateful; we'll be real glad to see her again," she reported.

Elizabeth added, "Now we'll get to see Jesse at last." Jesse was her little son whom we had never seen.

"When will they be here?"

"When, when?"

"Grace's letter says they will arrive around the first of July; in the meantime we have much to do. We'll have to get busy and clean house, especially the Sunday Room for them to sleep in," replied Mother, with her thoughts racing ahead. The Sunday Room was the one over the parlor and reserved for company only.

Grace's visit was the subject of conversation for the next several days, especially at mealtime. But at the supper table one evening, Pappy made an announcement that ignited our emotions, causing them to explode and pop like a dry hickory log thrown on a roaring fire.

"We'll be starting our wheat harvest in a day or so, the weather permitting. We have something to tell you children. Your mother and I have been discussing it for a long time, and we have decided that if we have a good wheat crop this year, we can perhaps afford to buy a car."

The sparks flew!

"Whoopee, whoopee! Oh boy, oh boy!" in one great chorus, interrupting Pappy.

Supper was forgotten almost completely, and our voices rose higher and higher, as we vied with each other to be heard.

"I guess now the Pences can be just as much as the Crows or anybody else! It won't make any difference if we are Dutch," I boasted.

Jake added, "And I guess now we can junk that old surrey, it is about ready to fall to pieces anyway."

"Pappy, when can I drive the new car?" Wilbur queried eagerly.

Pappy replied both humorously and sagely, "When you are old enough for long pants and when you can grow some whiskers, I suppose. One can't be too careful when he gets behind the wheel of those machines; they say some of them will go forty or fifty miles an hour. That's pretty fast traveling!"

Bertha, teasingly, said, "Watch Wilbur put some cream on his lips and let Old Tom lick it off, to make his whiskers grow. We'd better hide the cream."

"Aw, Bertha, cut that out! Mother, make Bertha hush up!"

"When will we get the car, Pappy?" asked Mary.

Ruth, when she had an opportunity to get in a word, said, "Maybe we can get it soon so we can take some trips before I go away to school in the fall."

"Yeah, I'd like to go to Harrisonburg sometime," suggested Frances.

With my bigger ideas, I added, "Or maybe we can go to Staunton or Charlottesville, I sure would like to go to East Virginia and see those big mansions we read about in our history book."

Pappy, cautioning us, said, "Whoa now, don't make too big plans or you'll have it worn out before it comes. We might get it after we cut the wheat and before we thresh, if the crop looks promising."

More yells and shouts!

Elizabeth thoughtfully suggested, "It will be nice to have it when Grace and Charlie get here."

The thoughts of a new car kept us enthusiastic and in high spirits, with no artificial stimulation in the days that followed.

The time came when Pappy and Jasper went to town with a neighbor to purchase the new machine and drive it home. Undoubtedly, this was the longest day of the year, but finally they drove in the road gate with Jasper sitting stiffly at the wheel. What a beautiful machine it was; our new Maxwell! We patted it and rubbed its slick surface; we climbed in and out, trying out the smooth leather seats! This was a proud day! After we had satisfied ourselves that it was for real, and that all bolts and nuts were in place, Jasper then drove it in the wagon shed.

We rode in the new auto at every available opportunity, whether to the store, church, or somewhere on other business. My joy was fulfilled, however, when Frances and I were chosen to take the trip across the mountain to Charlottesville and East Virginia. It was a girlhood dream come true! I had little eye for the virgin forest land as we crossed the Blue Ridge Mountain and dipped into the valley beyond. My eyes were scanning the landscape for red brick houses with white columns; and beautiful ladies in long full skirts enjoying their leisure as they sipped lemonade under the shade trees, while servants performed the chores. Mother had to hold onto my skirt tail to keep me from falling over the side of our open car when I beheld the first one. It was as lovely as I had visioned in my daydreams, though I confess, I didn't see the fine ladies with solicitous servants hovering over them. I had often projected myself vicariously into this role, and now I was determined that some day I would live it in reality. Someday, I would marry a Virginia Blueblood, live in my mansion and have servants to do the work: pick the beans, milk the cows, and scrub the floors. I would never reveal that I was of Dutch ancestry; that would be my deep dark secret locked in my mind for ever and ever. My dreams had not completely moved into the twentieth century.

I said to Frances, "I'd like to live in a house like that sometime."

She replied, "I wouldn't; it's too big and I would have too much work to do to clean it up."

"Dummy, you'd have servants to do that."

At that moment my attention was captured by another sight.

"Mother, what is that big round building over there and the other low brick buildings with it?"

"That's the University of Virginia, Thomas Jefferson's school."

"I'd like to go to school there sometime," I said wistfully.

"That school is only for boys!"

"Why?"

"I don't know, Esther, except I suppose it is more important for a boy to get an education than a girl."

"Why is it more important?"

"Boys support the family. That's the way life is," replied Mother trying to explain the relative status of men and women.

Somehow, these answers didn't completely satisfy my "Whys"; but my thoughts began to revert to other purposes and ambitions in life so the subject was forgotten.

The week following saw us making an initial readiness for Grace and family.

One morning, Mother said, "Girls, I think we'll churn today; that way we'll have a supply of butter to begin with. I've collected enough cream. Esther, you and Frances get yourselves ready for churning."

Her announcement had been so spontaneous and unanticipated by me, that I was trapped with no opportunity to find a niche out of sight and hearing. So the wooden churn in the cellar was duly filled with cream—hopefully at the right temperature so that the butter would come soon. Frances and I were stationed by it to alternate times at turning the handle connected to the dasher or paddles inside, to bring the butter.

Mother instructed, "Now turn it smoothly and evenly, not too fast and not too slow, each count to fifty and then the other can take over. Esther, you begin."

"One, two, three, four, five, six——" as I tried to synchronize my counting and turning.

Next Frances, "One two, three, four, five, six——fifty. Now it's your turn, Esther."

After lifting the lid and peeping in to see if there was any change in the looks of the cream that would indicate butter, "One, two, three, five, six, ten, twelve——"

"Esther, you're not countin' right! I'm gonna' tell Mother!"

Frances was by now advanced enough in years to count, and old enough in experience to be aware of the tricks I might try to pull.

"All right, all right, blabber mouth! One, two, three, four, five, six, seven——," correctly on to fifty.

Finally, the sloshing sound that indicated the butter was coming could be heard.

"Frances, run and tell Mother that it's done."

Frances quickly complied and soon returned with Mother, who lifted the lid and looked in.

"Yes, the butter is coming, but let's churn it a little more to gather it."

With a few more turns, it was sloshed into big lumps with some fragments left in the residue which was now buttermilk instead of cream. Mother reached in, gathered the large lumps in her hand and dropped them onto a large-sized meat platter. After straining the buttermilk to collect the small fragments as it flowed from the bunghole at the bottom of the churn, she carried the plate with its contents to the kitchen where Bertha took over. Bertha kneaded out all the buttermilk and worked in a little salt for flavoring. She then molded it into prints in the wooden butter mold, making it ready for storage and then usage.

Bread and butter! Butter and bread! The two go together. So it was that after butter making, we followed with bread making on the very next day.

The first step in this process was to set the yeast the night before. In setting the yeast, we mixed cooked potatoes and a quart of yeast saved from the previous baking, in lukewarm water. After this had been stirred together, we again removed a quart of this mixture for future baking—a continuous process.

On the following morning, Mother said, "I think it's about time for Esther to learn how to make bread. Elizabeth, maybe you can supervise her in that."

Elizabeth and I took a large dishpan to the flour chest which sat in the pantry and sifted it one-half to two-thirds full of flour. When back in the kitchen, we made a huge crater in the center and poured in the lukewarm yeast mixture, then added some soft lard for shortening. With my hands, I began gradually to work the flour into this liquid making it become thicker and thicker. By and by, I had a great hunk of soft spongy dough. When it reached the point of being no longer sticky, I emptied the excess flour back into the flour chest, greased the container, and placed my lump of dough back into it. Then I covered this with a clean towel and set it near the stove to raise.

Elizabeth advised, "Now Esther, you must check once in a while, and when the dough is about twice the size it is now, you must work it out into loaves."

I tried very carefully to follow Elizabeth's instructions as I wanted my first efforts in bread making to be successful. When the time came, I greased the voluminous black tin baking pans, worked down the great puffed-up hunk of bread dough, and formed it into ten loaves. Later the kitchen was filled with the aroma of freshly baking bread. In the evening, I stored the cooled loaves in the large tin boiler and shoved this under the kitchen table in its usual place.

We had the first taste of my product at supper that evening and Mother generously remarked, "Esther, your bread tastes mighty good."

Charlie, who was now home on vacation and still enjoyed kidding, said, "Golly, if Esther had her hands in this bread, I don't think I wanta' eat any of it."

But I observed that the bread plate was well emptied by the end of the meal—so my ego was satisfied.

Not many days later, Jasper drove our Maxwell to the train station at Grottoes to pick up our sister Grace, her husband, and young son. This was the sister I scarcely knew, but who so quickly became again a very natural and normal part of our family. There were times when it was questionable whether the house could sustain the turbulence, the clamor, the explosions produced by eleven children, two parents, a son-in-law and a grandchild, or whether it would convulse with one last gasp. Perhaps the floors and steps became a bit more creaky; the walls and timbers somewhat fractured; the roof raised a little higher, but we simply were not aware.

The big black cookstove carried a heavier load of pots and pans filled with new potatoes, corn on the cob, beans, cabbage, and stewing apples. Our dining room table regularly had Pappy at the head, five on each side, two at the end facing Pappy, and Frances and I were learning to eat off the corners. The only moments of quietness were when Pappy said the blessing. When he ended with the "Amen," conversation began, along with the passing of food down, around, up, with the one at the end of the line hoping the contents of the dishes would last until they reached him.

Mother, seizing an opportunity to speak, said, "Let's see now, tomorrow we get beef. That's right, isn't it?"

Pappy answered, "Yes, that's right. Mr. Saufley butchers this time. He usually has pretty good beef."

"I'm glad we're getting beef while Grace is here. It will come in mighty good to have some now," added Mother.

The beef, to which they were referring, was the result of a company organized by a group of farmers in the area. The company was composed of eight members who took turns butchering fattened beeves on alternating weeks through the summer months. All members received their proportionate share of meat at each slaughtering—perhaps the beginning of the co-op? Lacking an electric refrigerator or wooden ice chest, we stored a part of the beef in Grandpap Harshbarger's icehouse, sunk low in the ground, and filled with ice that had been cut from the "cricks" during the cold winter months; then covered with sawdust to prevent melting. When we desired a mess of this stored meat, a couple of us girls were dispatched the two miles to fetch it from the depths of sawdust and ice.

Saturday at this period was pandemonium day: house-cleaning, baking, preparing other foods for the day of worship and rest that followed. Baths began early in the afternoon and continued into the night, for fifteen human bodies.

Grace, calling to Frances and me, said, "Girls, before your bathtime comes, we have a job for you. Elizabeth would like to have some daisies picked to fill two crocks she wants to put on the front porch. She is expecting her beau tomorrow evening and wants things to look nice. Maybe Jesse can go with you."

With Jesse between us, we crossed the road into the field of daisies—God's florist shop—and began gathering the yellow and white posies.

"Jesse, don't pull them off by their heads like that; they aren't any good that way!" I scolded.

Frances, sometime later, asked, "Don't ya' think we have enough?"

"I don't know but I hope so; let's go and see."

Grace was waiting on the front porch with two crocks of water, as we appeared. "Girls, I'm sorry but this is not nearly enough."

So back to the field we went. We certainly had no idea that one crock could hold so many! By the time we had finally satisfied Grace with the quantity we had picked, we were ready for our baths without persuasion or pressure.

The time came when Grace and family bade us good-by and returned to their home; Charlie returned to his job. We bounced down to a little more routine living, if it were ever possible to live routinely on our farm.

Among the materials that were diminished or depleted through the days when our family was increased, was our supply of homemade soap. So now, Mother decided it was necessary to restock. A sufficient amount of fat and grease had been collected.

The twenty-five gallon black iron kettle in the wash-house had multiple functions, and now again it was being put to use. Mother put all the grease and fat meat scraps into the kettle over the heat along with a little water. Then lastly, she carefully added a can of lye or caustic soda which reacted with the fat and saponified. We stirred it as it gurgled and bubbled like the Yellowstone mudpots, while the water was being cooked out.

As I was doing my turn at stirring the burpy, yellowish brown mixture, Mary came to the back porch and yelled, "Esther-r-r! Elizabeth B. wants you on the phone."

More than glad to shift the stirring stick to Bertha, I sped to the house on flying feet. In a matter of seconds I dashed back to the washhouse, "Mother! Elizabeth wants us to come over this evening after supper! Cousin Otis has finished puttin' their radio together and they want us to come and listen to it! She says it's really somethin' to hear voices comin' through the air into that box without any wires to come on! Do they really do that Mother?"

"I don't know; I haven't heard it, but that's what they say. I suppose you all can go over for awhile this evening."

I hurried again to the telephone to relay the good news to Elizabeth. My feet weren't flying this time as I meandered back to the washhouse and the kettle of boiling soap mixture. Luckily for me, by the time I finally appeared in the door again, the stirring operation was concluded.

After this mixture began to cool, the soap formed and solidified on top, leaving a residue in the bottom. Mother then cut into blocks this solid top layer and stored it away for future washing and bathing needs.

When our "evening time" arrived we scampered along the road and up the path that led to the Bowman's house. This was an opportunity to experience a marvel of communication, maybe once in a lifetime, for we had no concept of its future potential.

Upon taking a look at the long wooden box with several dials across the front, Jake asked, "You gonna' tell me that you can hear talkin' and music in that thing from a long way off?"

Margaret, cocksure with experience replied, "You sure can, Jake! I wouldn't believe it either 'til I heard it. Here, you all put on these earphones and listen."

Cousin Otis had installed two sets of these on his radio. Rather skeptically we put them over our ears, yet to be convinced that a miracle in sound would come to us.

Jake and Wilbur, with questionable expertness, were going over the box from front to back as if they were searching for a voice concealed somewhere inside. They could see only a set of batteries, some wires and little lights, and other gadgets that meant little to their unknowledgeable minds.

When my turn came to listen I clumsily adjusted the headphones over my ears.

"I hear some music playing!" I screamed excitedly.

After listening a minute, "Now they said this is Station KDKA Pittsburgh! What does that mean?"

I was not interested in an answer and I couldn't hear them anyway with the headphones over my ears, so I continued, "Hey! Somebody just said somethin' about Warren G. Harding bein' in Omaha, Nebraska, today talkin' to people."

Wilbur, grabbing my earphones, said, "I wanta' listen if they are talkin' about politics!"

Frances, as she listened, asked, "Do you think that is comin' from heaven? Maybe that's God talkin'!"

Wilbur, with adolescent humor, scoffed, "Huh! When I put my hand on something inside this box, it felt hot, so I don't think it could be comin' from heaven!" He continued, "I read somewhere that they are sayin' they will be able to send pictures over the air someday!"

"I bet that'll never happen!" said Margaret.

Unaware of what the future might bring, this here and now moment had brought a new world of sound into our lives.

CHAPTER 10

CONFESSION-COMMUNION

Summer began to wane, but not the chores and activities of our farm. The most important event of late summer was the revival, or "big meeting," that was held annually at our church. This particular "big meeting" was something of a milestone in my young life—for this was the year I made the decision to join the church. Joining the church in my community was not a difficult decision to make. I had no moving experience; the Holy Spirit was gentle with me—not disturbing my emotions greatly, but led me to this decision in the way I was led to make other decisions later in life. Neither was I impelled to enumerate the sins I had committed and to repent of them in one great moment of confession and ablution. Rather, it was a pattern of life for the young people, including my brothers and sisters, to unite with the church sometime in the adolescent period. We had been taught since early childhood, that the only way to be saved was through the doors of the church. This is not to say that the exhortations of the evangelist: to repent and be baptized, save yourself from hell and damnation, and assure your entry someday into the gates of heaven, did not have their emotional effect. Indeed, we had some rather graphic pictures in our minds of the fiery horrors of "the bad place," and of white robed angels in an ethereal realm of eternal bliss. Thus, after such a sermon, followed by the singing of one or two invitational hymns, such as "Just As I Am," or "Why Not Tonight?," the emotions of young life came into play, to a degree. Therefore, it was not difficult for me to leave my seat near the front as I had previously planned, walk the short distance up the aisle and give my hand to the preacher and my heart to God.

No great emotional experience actually came to me later when my Pappy baptized me in Mill Creek, not far from our church. Yet it seems to me wholly good, that life in the church for me and my brothers and sisters began in such a way.

Our church had something of a natural order, or at least, an order of events. The one that followed the series of meetings and preceding communion, was known as "The Deacons' Visitation," the purpose of which was to prepare members for the services of Communion and The Lord's Supper. These events took on great significance for me since I was now a member of the fellowship. I went willingly when Mother dispatched Frances and me to round up the men from the fields, as two deacons (Brother Hartman and Brother Cline) drove up to our front gate. I never felt more grown-up or more proud, than in the moment I sat in the front room, my prayer cap atop my head along with my mother and sisters, in the presence of our menfolk and solemnly answered "Yes" to the three questions asked us by the visiting deacons:

1. Are you still in the faith of the gospel as you were when you were baptized?
2. As far as you know, are you at peace with everybody, especially the members of the church?
3. Are you still willing to work for an increase in holiness both in yourself and others?

As the deacons were ready to depart, Brother Hartman turned to Mother and asked, "Sister Pence, have you made arrangements to make bread for communion on Saturday?"

She answered in the affirmative.

Friday afternoon a group of the sisters of the church in their homemade cotton dresses and aprons were seated around our dining room table with its newly scrubbed oilcloth cover. Their hair was pinned back neatly in buns

147

on the tops or backs of their heads, revealing placid ruddy faces.

On the table in front of each was a hunk of communion bread dough. Mother had mixed this by an age-old recipe, plenty of cream and butter, but no salt or leavening. They chattered and kneaded, and kneaded and chattered, for the traditional recipe said "until it blistered and squeaked"; and they appeared never to lack the patience and fortitude to bring it to that stage. This seemed like an interminable length of time to us children, who were waiting around to sample the finished product—the taste was delicious.

Finally, Elizabeth B. and I, losing our patience with this slow process, left the dining room. As we walked across the porch, Elizabeth spied a bucket of somewhat green fall apples that had been brought in from the orchard for pie baking, and suggested, "Gee, they look good; let's take some of them with us."

Enough said, so we each snitched a handful and mosied out to the old dilapidated buggy behind the chicken shed, and stepped up and in. As we sat on the seat and began gnawing on the hard little green apples, we bounced up and down on the seat with vigor and emphasis. To our delight, the springs propelled us higher with each jump and bounce, and carried the green apples to the nether regions of our alimentary canals.

I asked Elizabeth, who had joined the church the previous year, "Are you better than you were before you joined the church?"

She replied, "I don't know, but I try to do better, for I sure don't want to be burned up in the bad place like the preacher said we would if we didn't repent."

"I want to go to heaven too, but how do you know when you are good enough? I don't know whether I have any great big sins or not, but maybe I have some little ones, like telling stories, and fussing, and acting ugly. I'm anxious to go to communion tomorrow. It's not much fun to sit on those raised seats every year and watch others eat the beef and bread soup, sip the grape juice, and break the strips of bread for each other."

Never any fermented beverages in our church, and the day had not arrived for individual communion glasses to replace the "Common Cup."

Elizabeth suggested, "Let's sit together if our mothers will let us, but don't you laugh when we kiss after we wash feet. If you do, then you'll get me tickled."

Philosophical subjects were soon forgotten, however, as we slipped into the house for the discarded trimmings from the edges of freshly baked communion bread, and brought it back to munch on with our green apples.

But going to church for my first communion the next day was not to be, for when morning came, I awoke with a bellyache and vomiting. Perhaps it was God's judgment on me for eating too many green apples and rich communion bread, or for one of the other sins of which I knew I was guilty, but had not confessed.

So it was that sister Elizabeth remained at home with me that sorrowful day. By late evening, I felt better and decided to try my legs and tummy outdoors for awhile. I strolled to the newly mown hayfield behind the house, and there I could see our part of the valley laid out between two great mountain ranges, the Allegheny and Blue Ridge. The Massanutten, jutting only part way up this valley, seemed to have been God's afterthought. At this moment I stood also between girlhood and womanhood, and my thoughts seemed to be on a teeter totter as I began to wonder about life. Would one always be faced with hardships and frustrations as I had today? Or would my dreams someday come true? Would the time come when I could learn more about the universe with its mountains that surrounded me, or would I too, like my mother, have my formal schooling cut short and find my lot on a farm with a large family to care for? Would life always be full of disappointments; or would I live happily everafter as in the romances I had read?

Only the years to follow could answer those questions for me.

CHAPTER 11

AFTER YEARS

Families do not remain self-contained units forever on self-contained farms forever. Families come into being and families go out of being; others are born and take their places. Children grow into adulthood and follow their aspirations and dreams. The remnant that is left at home when this process begins witnesses the effects more poignantly when the ties are broken.

It was the summer of Ruth's wedding day. Frances and I had once more gathered daisies and honeysuckle from the fields to entwine the arch under which she and her betrothed would take their vows. However, this time we picked a much lesser quantity—arches do not hold as many as crocks. We liked and accepted her choice as a husband. He seemed like a fine, upstanding, young man.

"But gee whiz!" I thought, "Why did he have to be a Dutchman?"

Somehow, beginning with this event, it seemed that the family ties were being severed rapidly and irrevocably.

Elizabeth, whom we thought was destined to be a career woman and an old maid after so many years of exercising a rather fastidious and definite taste, finally found matrimony alluring.

Grace, of course, had long since been settled in her home and was performing her duties as wife and mother.

Charlie had definitely decided on his future course away from the farm and in the big city, where he, no doubt, helped enliven any situation in which he became involved.

And our Bertha, always looking to the future with buoyancy and optimism, had concluded her teacher training and was now happily established in this profession.

Wilbur and Mary had completed the school at Timber Ridge, and would leave home in the fall to finish their high school studies and move on to further pursuits. In spite of his great interest in history, Wilbur never became an historian, a great Napoleonic warrior, or even a career soldier.

The remnant left on the farm was the most keenly aware of the breakup. This remnant included the three young members of the family—Jake, Frances, and me—along with Jasper, now established there, and our Mother and Pappy. The young trio was already looking forward to a year or two hence, when they, also, would follow Wilbur and Mary to further educational and career pursuits.

The occupants of the old home are gone now, but the house and barn still remain. The woods, the meadows, the fields are there too; yet something is missing, gone, departed, passed away. But voices of times past must still echo through the house and the barn: the laughter and shouts of children at work and play; the admonitions of a Mother and Pappy who watched over them. Forms must still be roaming over those fields, the meadows, and flitting through the woods; their bare feet running over the hills, calling to neighbors to come and play. They tell the story of a family who was there a long time and yet so short time ago, a living breathing family of eleven children with their Mother and Pappy.

The days of our childhood often seem an eternity; but the ensuing days and years come tumbling in at supersonic speed. And so it was with the girl in this story. Some of my ambitions, hopes, and dreams became realities; others never came to fruition, which no doubt is just as well.

The nebulous, faceless, formless figure of my Prince Charming became substance and reality.

And now I, Esther Virginia Pence Garber, do herewith make this confession, signed, sealed, witnessed to this day in the Shenandoah Valley of the State of Virginia:

I married a Dutchman.

P. S.: I never did get those button shoes.

GLOSSARY

BANKS OF CLOUDY

1. 'Twas on one sum-mer's even-ing, And in the Month of May.
Out in a flow-ery gar-den Young Bet-tie, she did stray.
Young Bet-tie, she did stray, Young Bet-tie, she did stray.
Out in a flow-ery gar-den Young Bet-tie, she did stray.

2. I stepped up to this fair maid
   And took her by surprise.
   I own she did not know me,
   I being in disguise.

3. Said I, "My charming creature;
   My joy and heart's delight,
   How far have you to travel
   This dark and rainy night?"

4. "The way kind Sir, to Cloudy;
   If you will please to show.
   Oh pity a maid distracted,
   There's where I wish to go!"

5. "I'm searching for a young man,
   And Johnnie is his name;
   And on the banks of Cloudy
   I'm told he does remain."

6. "If Johnnie were here this night
   He'd keep me from all harm.
   But he is on the battlefield,
   All in his uniform."

7. "He's on the battlefield.
   His foes he will destroy,
   Like the raging wings of Homer
   When he fought the wars of Troy."

154

8. "He is on the wide ocean
   For honor and for gain.
   The last we heard the ship was wrecked
   Along the coast of Spain."

9. When she heard the dreadful news,
   She fell into despair;
   With wringing of her lily-white hands,
   And the tearing of her hair.

10. "And now he's gone and left me,
    No man on earth I'll take.
    But in some lonely vallie
    I wander for his sake."

11. His heart was filled with joy;
    He could no longer stand,
    But flew into her arms
    Saying, "Bettie, I am the man!"

12. "I am that faithless young man
    Whom ye thought was slain,
    And since we've met on Cloudy's Banks,
    We'll never part again."

1. "No home! No home!" cried the lit-tle girl, as she stood at the prin-ce's door.

"Won't you give me a home?" she fee-bly said, "A home and a crust of bread?"

2. "My father, Sir, I never knew,"
   And the tears in her eyes shone bright.
   "My mother she sleeps in a new-made grave;
   'Tis an orphan that begs tonight."

3. The rich man slept in his velvet bed,
   And dreamed of his silver and gold.
   But the little girl lay on her bed of snow
   And murmured, "So cold, so cold!"

4. The morning dawned on the little girl,
   As she lay at the marble hall.
   But her spirit had fled to the mansions above,
   Where there's room and bread for all.

POOR OLD MAIDS

1. Dressed in yel-low, pink, and blue— Poor old maids!

Dressed in yel-low, pink, and blue— Poor old maids!

Dressed in yel-low, pink, and blue, not a string in ei-ther shoe,

Nurs-ing cats is all we do, Poor old maids!

2. Off to the meeting we will go -
   Poor old maids!
   Off to the meeting we will go -
   Poor old maids!
   Off to the meeting we will go -
   Through the rain and through the snow,
   'Spectin' there to catch a beau,
   Poor old maids!

3. When we get there we'll sit down -
   Poor old maids!
   When we get there we'll sit down -
   Poor old maids!
   When we get there we'll sit down -
   Boys, they'll all begin to frown,
   And our faces wrinkle down,
   Poor old maids!

4. When the devil gets his due -
   Poor old maids!
   When the devil gets his due -
   Poor old maids!
   When the devil gets his due -
   Take along those bachelors too!
   Take along those bachelors too!
   Poor old maids!

157

WE'VE GOT THE MUMPS !

Oh, yes! We've got the mumps, all right; the wor-sest kind of

mumps. And if you don't take care of us you certainly are chumps. For

if you don't you'll get exposed; That's what the doctor said. And

it's not any fun, you bet, to have a swelled - up head; To

have a swelled - up head!

TWENTY YEARS AGO

1. How won-.drous are the chan-ges Since twen-ty years a-go! When girls wore wool-len dres-ses; and boys wore pants of tow; When shoes were made of cow-hide, and socks from home-spun wool, And chil-dren did a half day's work Be-fore they went to school.

CHORUS:

Just twenty years ago, Just twenty years ago, the men and the boys and the girls and the .toys, The work and the play and the night and the day, The

world and its ways are all turned round, Since twen - ty years a - go....

2. The girls took music lessons Upon the spinning wheel,
   And practised late and early On spindle, swift and reel.
   The boys would ride the horse to mill A dozen miles or
   so,
   And hurry off before 'twas day, Some twenty years ago.
   (CHORUS)

3. The people rode to meeting In sleds instead of sleighs;
   And wagons rode as easy As buggies now a-days;
   And oxen answered well for teams, Though now they'd
   be too slow,
   For people lived not half so fast, Some twenty years ago.
   (CHORUS)

4. Oh! Well do I remember That Wilson's patent stove,
   That father bought and paid for In cloth our girls had
   wove;
   And how the neighbors wondered When we "got the
   thing" to go,
   And said " 'twould burst" and kill us all, Some twenty
   years ago.
   (CHORUS)

5. Yes, ev'ry thing is altered, I cannot tell the cause,
   For men are always tamp'ring With nature's wondrous
   laws;
   And what on earth we're coming to - Does anybody
   know?
   For everything has changed so much Since twenty
   years ago.
   (CHORUS)

From *Star of Bethlehem*: Ruebush-Kieffer Company, Copyright 1889.

CARVE THAT POSSUM

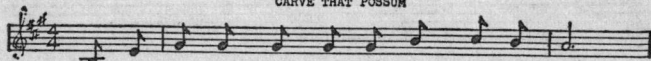

Carve that pos - sum, carve that pos - sum, Hee! Hee! Hee!

He is still a - sit - tin' in the old par - sim - mon tree.

'Nough to make a fel - ler's mouth wat - ter cl'ar ov - er thar

When he thinks of coon legs, pos - sum fat or b'ar.

Carve that pos-sum, carve that pos-sum, carve him fa'r (carve him fa'r)!

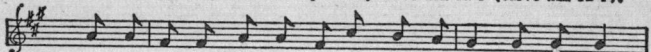

Carve that po - po - po - po - pos-sum, carve him fa'r (carve him fa'r)!

Give me shoul-der, back-bone, and the neck and ribs (carve him fa'r)!

And I'll 'low you all the tail and the ha'r (carve him fa'r)!

161

KING WILLIAM

King Wil-liam was King James's son, All the roy-al race he won.

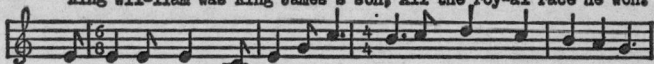

Up-on his breast he wore a star That was called the life of war.

Go choose your east, Go choose your west, Go choose the one

that you love best. If she's not here to take her part, Choose

the next one to your heart. Down up-on this car-pet you must

kneel, Sure's the grass grows in the field. Sa-lute your bride

and kiss her sweet. Rise a - gain up - on your feet.

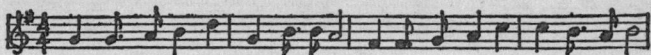

1. Twilight is stealing over the sea; Shadows are falling dark on the lea.

Borne on the nightwinds, voices of yore, come from the far-off shore.

CHORUS:

Far away beyond the starlit skies, where the lovelight never, never dies,

Gleameth a mansion filled with delight, sweet, happy home, so bright!

2. Voices of loved ones! Songs of the past!
   Still linger around me while life shall last.
   Lonely I wander, sadly I roam, seeking that far-off
   home.

   (CHORUS)

3. Come in the twilight, come, come to me,
   bringing some message over the sea.
   Cheering my pathway while here I roam, seeking that
   far-off home.

   (CHORUS)

B.C. Unseld arrangement, from *The Temple Star:* Ruebush-Kieffer Company.

1. Look down this lone green val-ley Where the vio-lets bloom and fade,

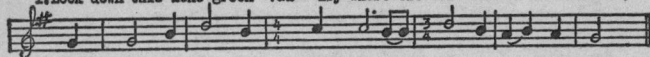

There's where my sweet Flo - rel - la Lies mold-ing in her grave.

2. She died not broken hearted,
   Nor from disease she fell;
   But in a moment parted
   From all she loved so well.

3. One night the moon shone brightly;
   And the stars were shining too,
   When to her lonely cottage
   Her jealous lover drew.

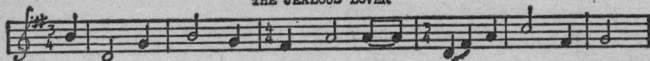

4. Said he, "Come, Love, let's wander
   Out in the night so gay.
   Of wandering we will ponder
   Upon our wedding day."

5. So out into the forest,
   He led his love so dear.
   Said she, " 'Tis far to wander
   When all is dark and drear."

6. "The night grows dark and dreary,
   And I'm afraid to stay
   Of wandering I am weary
   And will retrace my way."

7. "Retrace your way, no never,
   For you not far to roam,
   For soon to bid farewell
   To parents, friends, and home."

8. Down on her knees before him
   She pleaded for her life;
   But deep into her bosom
   He plunged that fatal knife.

9. "Dear Willie, I'll forgive you,"
   Was her last and dying breath,
   "I never have deceived you,"
   And she closed her eyes in death.

10. The banners waved about her
    In a faint and bugle sound;
    The strangers came and found her
    Cold and lifeless on the ground.

1. Mis - ses Lof - ty has her car - riage; So do I. She has
dap - ple greys to draw it; None have I. She's no proud - er
with her coach - man, than am I. with my laugh - ing
blue - eyed bab - y trund - ling by. I hide his
face, lest she should see the che - rub boy and en - vy me.

2. Her fine husband has white fingers;
   Mine has not.
   He could give his bride a palace;
   Mine a cot.
   Her husband comes in the evening
   Ne'er cares she.
   Mine comes in the purple twilight;
   Kisses me,
   And prays that He who turns life's sands
   Will hold his loved ones in His hands.

3. Mrs. Lofty has her station;
   So do I.
   Hers is money, mine is love;
   Glad am I!
   I'd not trade it for a kingdom;
   No not I!
   God will weigh it in his balance
   By and by.
   For I have love, and she has gold;
   She counts her wealth, mine can't be told.

4. Mrs. Lofty has her jewels;
   So do I.
   She wears hers upon her bosom;
   Inside, I.
   She will leave hers at death's portals
   By and by.
   I shall bear my treasure with me
   When I die.
   And then the difference will define
   Twixt Mrs. Lofty's wealth and mine.

LILLY-O

1. There lived a rich old merchant, In London he did dwell. He had a lovely daughter, Her name to you I'll tell, Lilly - O, O Lilly, Lilly - O.

2. This lady she was courted
By men of high degree;
But none but Jack the Sailor
Could climb the raging sea.
Lilly-O O, Lilly, Lilly-O.

3. Poor Jackie's gone a - sailing
With a sad and troubled mind;
The leaving of his country,
His darling girl behind.
Lilly-O O, Lilly, Lilly-O.

4. She stepped right down to the tailor's shop
And dressed in men's array,
And listed as a soldier
To take herself away.
Lilly-O O, Lilly, Lilly-O.

5. Before you go on board, sir,
Your name I'd like to know;
A-smiling in her countenance,
They call me Jack Monroe.
Lilly-O O, Lilly, Lilly-O.

6. And when the war was ended
She took a search around,
And among the dead and wounded,
Her darling Jack she found.
Lilly-O O, Lilly, Lilly-O.

7. She picked him up into her arms
   And to the city fled
   To hunt of some physician
   Her warrior's wound to cure.
   Lilly-O O, Lilly, Lilly-O.

8. So that couple, they got married,
   So well did they agree.
   That couple, they got married,
   It's why don't you and me?
   Lilly-O O, Lilly, Lilly-O.

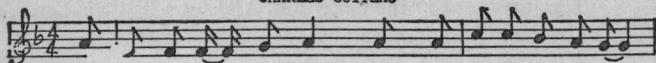

Come, all you ten - der Chris - tians, Wher-ev-er you may be,

And like - wise pay at - ten - tion To these few lines from me.

'Twas on the twen - tieth of June, I was con - demned to die

For the mur-der of James A. Gar-field, Up-on the scaf-fold high.

(CHORUS)

My name is Charles Gui - teau; My name I'll never de - ny,

But I leave my ag - ed par - ents In sor - row for to die.

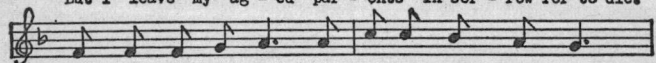

Lit - tle did I think, When in my youth - ful bloom,

I'd be tak-en to the scaf - fold to meet my fa - tal doom.

2. I went down to the depot, I tried to make my escape.
   But Providence against me, It proved to be too late.
   I tried to play insane, But I saw it would not do.
   The people all around me, It proved to be no show.
   (CHORUS)

3. My sister came to prison To bid her last farewell.
   She threw her arms around me And wept most bitterly.
   She says, "Brother, Dear, Today you must die
   For the murder of James A. Garfield Upon the scaffold
   high!"   (CHORUS)

4. 'Twas on the day of my trial, As you may plainly see,
   The jury went in the backroom And soon they did agree.
   The jury found me guilty; The judge made this reply,
   "On the twenty-third of August, You are condemned
   to die."   (CHORUS)

The hangman is a-waiting; 'Tis a quarter after two.
5. Oh! Now I am on the scaffold; I bid you all adieu.
   The black cap over my face, No longer can I see.
   And when I'm dead and buried, Good Lord, remember
   me!   (CHORUS)

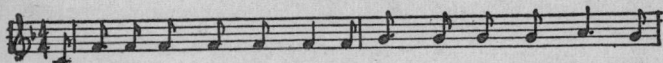

1. I saw a way-worn trav'-ler in tat-tered gar-ments clad. And
strug-gling up the moun-tain, it seemed that he was sad. His
back was lad-en heav-y, his strength was al-most gone; Yet
shout-ed as he jour-neyed, "De-liv-er-ance will come!"

CHORUS:
Then palms of vic-tor-y, crowns of glo-ry, palms of vic-to-ry I shall wear.

2. I saw him in the evening; The sun was bending low;
   Had overtopped the mountain And reached the vale
      below.
   He saw the golden city, His everlasting home,
   And shouted loud, "Hosanna! Deliverance will come!"
                                              (Chorus)

3. While gazing on that city, Just o'er the narrow flood,
   A band of holy angels Came from the Throne of God.
   They bore him on their pinions, Safe o'er the dashing
      foam,
   And joined him in his triumph - "Deliverance has come!"
                                              (Chorus)

From: PEARLS OF TRUTH, Ruebush-Kieffer Company, Copyright 1890.